Among the Shadows

Among the Shadows

EDITED BY
DEMITRIA LUNETTA
KATE KARYUS QUINN
MINDY McGINNIS

Table of Contents

Introduction

YOU'VE BEEN THERE.

It's dark and you're comfortable. You're just about to fall asleep when you can't help but wonder if maybe tonight the thing you've always been sure exists will finally find you.

The best short stories stick with you, and the stories in this book especially are meant to cast long shadows. The authors who contributed to this anthology are not only familiar with what lurks among the shadows, we choose to spend time there. Our monsters all live in different places—under beds, beside peaceful streams, inside ourselves, down mine shafts, in the sky. The darkness you'll find in these pages knows no boundaries, so it's only fitting that these stories cover many genres.

Reality can be just as terrifying as anything our imaginations conjure, which is why the darkness in these pages isn't relegated just to flights of fancy or the paranormal. In choosing such a wide range of stories, our hope is that everyone will find something to make them clutch their bedcovers a little closer.

In realistic contemporary stories from Joelle Charbonneau and Kelly Fiore, depression, addiction, obsession, and isolation are all the stuff of nightmares. Other stories by Justina Ireland, Phoebe North, and Geoffrey Girard straddle the line, making us question what is real and what is false. Mindy McGinnis explores the question of not knowing yourself, while Kate Karyus Quinn speculates on the effect of learning that every terrible thing that's ever happened to you has been manufactured for the entertainment of others.

Demitria Lunetta and Gretchen McNeil each take a closer, horrific look at human nature. Lenore Applehans delves into a post-apocalyptic future, while R.C. Lewis discovers the darkness that lurks on another planet in her science fiction narrative. Then of course there are the paranormal stories from Beth Revis and Lydia Kang, each digging into the many types of monsters that might wait for us in the dark. Overall, you'll find a wide range of horrors represented, including demons, aliens, and one of the most frightening creatures ever—human beings.

So set aside an hour or two, switch on some lights and come join us . . . among the shadows.

The Eyes Have It

Gretchen McNeil

"How could you do this?" Jane screamed for what felt like the millionth time. Her voice was raw, her vocal cords shredded from the agitated mix of rage and hysterics.

She knew the question was futile—Ryan hadn't answered her the first nine hundred ninety-nine thousand nine hundred ninety-nine times, why would he now? But she couldn't help herself, as if launching the words at his stoic face would somehow lessen the pain.

"How could you cheat on me?"

Through a Vaseline lens of hot tears, she stared into her boyfriend's eyes, searching for some sign of remorse. Or regret. Or even pity. That would be an improvement over the blank stare. His eyes twitched back and forth across her face but like his lips, they said nothing.

Jane turned away, unable to bear his silence, and collapsed into a chair, face in her hands, weeping. She loved Ryan *so* much. SO MUCH. The ache emanating from the cavity beneath her ribcage was unbearable. As if she'd been stabbed, then shot, then lit on fire. How was she supposed to go on like this? Without him?

Ryan was her first boyfriend. Her first everything. She'd given every piece of herself to this relationship, and she'd been an absolutely perfect girlfriend, hadn't she? From the very beginning! She'd felt honored and special and singled out when he pursued her, desperate for a first date, refusing to take no for an answer. He'd been adorably embarrassed when he asked if she'd help him study. His lips said "Algebra test" but his eyes said "first date," as if he was too shy to actually ask her out.

But Jane knew what he meant. She'd noticed him watching her in the hallways, caught his eyes on her in the cafeteria. They were from totally different circles, but Ryan hadn't cared. He *wanted* her. That was love. That was passion! And after she finally agreed to "study" with him, she'd fallen desperately in love.

She adored Ryan, supported him in every girlfriendly way possible. Right? Who could have done more? She'd shown up at every cross country meet to cheer him along the rugged dirt trails, helped him with his Algebra and Chemistry and American History when he was afraid he was going to fail and get kicked off the team, written his papers on *Great Expectations* and *The*

Invisible Man because he didn't have time to do them himself.

Had she been mistaken? Had Ryan never cared at all?

No, he loved her too. She knew that. Truly, deeply *knew* it despite what he'd done with Brooke. She remembered that afternoon in his bedroom when he'd shoved the textbooks aside and whispered into her ear while he slid her shirt over her head. "You're beautiful, Jane." They had been completely alone for the first time; his parents were still at work, his little brother at a friend's house. It had felt dangerous and sexy, like she was breaking the rules. She recalled the thrill that had raced through her body as his fingers deftly unhooked her bra, then trailed lightly over her bare breasts.

She'd been nervous, unsure.

"*I love you, Jane.*" He'd pressed his body into her and she'd felt something hard against her thigh.

That's love. *True* love. Not the shallow feelings he had for Brooke Sanders, who was beautiful and perfect and envied by everyone at school. Including Jane, even before she'd barged into Ryan's bedroom and found Brooke on her knees before him, his head thrown back with a heavy moan escaping his lips.

Had Ryan told Brooke he loved her too?

"This can't be happening," Jane sobbed into the crook her arm. "You said you loved me."

Ryan made a noise that sounded exactly like "Mmhm."

Jane leapt to her feet, her sorrow forgotten. "You love me. I knew it. I knew you didn't love *her*. I knew you wanted to be with me forever and ever and whatever happened between you and Brooke was a mistake. No, not even! It was just a misunderstanding, right? She forced herself on you, didn't she? You were just trying to get rid of her when I got there."

Jane paused to take a quick breath, hoping Ryan might give her an answer. When he seemed content with silence, she pushed.

"I mean, you *knew* I'd be there any minute. To help you study for finals. It wasn't like you were doing any of this behind my back." She laughed nervously, excited by her own argument. "Yeah, that makes perfect sense. This was just a fluke. A one-time thing. Brooke tried to seduce you, and since you knew I was coming over, you were just . . ."

Her voice trailed off as Ryan's eyes shifted away. He couldn't look at her. Which meant everything she was saying was complete and utter bullshit.

"No," she said quietly, more calmly than she felt. "No, that's not true. You and Brooke had been together before, hadn't you?"

His eyes shifted back to her; they said more than words could ever convey. They were watery, pupils so wide only a thin rim of blueish gray remained, ringing them like a corona. The whites were tinged with red, thin veins creeping from the corners like hands grasping at the irises, and his eyelids were puffy and swollen and filled with guilt. His lips quivered, parting slightly as if he was about to say something. But then he chickened out, confirming all of Jane's worst fears.

He had been cheating on her with Brooke for quite some time.

While the enormity of this realization washed over her, a single tear threaded its way from the corner of Ryan's left eye, snaking around freckles as it raced toward his chin.

"You don't deserve to be sad, Ryan." She spit the words out, anger bubbling up inside her. "Get it? *I* get to cry. *I* get to feel as if my heart has cracked into two pieces and will never, ever be whole again for as long as I live. Not *you*."

A second tear gathered, racing after its sibling before it took a diverting turn and disappeared below his ear. Were these tears of regret? Tears of actual human feeling? Again, his lips twitched as if he was about to speak, and Jane knew exactly what he was going to say.

I'm so sorry.

"No!" Jane shrieked, cutting him off. She eyed the glistening trail the last tear had made on Ryan's cheek. There was no sadness in it. No sense of loss. Ryan's only remorse lay in the fact that he'd gotten caught.

So you know what? She didn't want to hear his apology because that would mean she'd have to consider forgiving him, if even for a split second. And she didn't want that thought to cross her mind. Because if it crossed her mind, she'd have to think about it. And

7

if she thought about it, she'd probably forgive him. How could she not? She loved him!

Jane took a deep breath to steady herself. She loved him. That was the beginning and the end of it. She. Loved. Him.

She turned back to Ryan feeling once more as if she could forgive him. "I just need to know you're sorry," she said, grasping his hand. "That it was a mistake and that you'll never, ever do it again."

She held her breath, waiting for those two little words to pass his lips: I'm sorry. Yes, she could forgive him! They could be happy again!

But instead of an apology, Ryan's eyes hardened, and in them Jane saw an accusation.

This is your fault.

Jane reared back, dropping his hand. Oh, hell no. This couldn't be her fault. At all. Had she forced him into Brooke's waiting arms? Had she held a gun to his head and forced him to submit to that blowjob? No freaking way.

You've been so busy lately. Unavailable. You missed the last two track meets of the year.

Jane gritted her teeth. Starting spring semester, Jane's parents had thought it would be a good idea for her to have a part-time job after school to earn extra money for college, and so she'd been forced to work in her dad's dental office. She was assigned a variety of menial, mind-numbing tasks that even a trained monkey could accomplish: filing, sterilizing equipment, answering the phones when the receptionist took her break, scanning documents, and other general busywork. A total waste of her time. Which made missing Ryan's track meets—including Regionals—even more frustrating.

It had sucked, but at the beginning, it hadn't seemed like a big deal. With the shift from fall to spring sports, Ryan was at track practice every day until at least five o'clock anyway. It wasn't like she was missing quality couple time.

But maybe he felt slighted? Abandoned? Maybe he felt like Jane didn't love him enough to spend all of her time with him?

And Brooke was there for me.

"That's not an excuse!" Jane yelled, the anger flaring up again. This time, minus the hot flood of tears. "You should have talked to me about it, shared your feelings. That's what grown-up couples do, Ryan. They don't just hop into bed with the first dumb slut who goes down on them."

She's not dumb. And she's not a slut.

Brooke Sanders. Homecoming Court, decent student, with a group of perfect friends who wore perfect clothes and drove perfect cars and had perfect jobless after-school lives. If she wasn't a dumb slut, then why had she messed around with a guy who already had a girlfriend? Had Ryan told her that he and Jane had broken up?

Jane caught her breath. Was Brooke innocent?

No way. Even if Ryan had lied, convincing Brooke that he had broken up with his girlfriend, she'd have to be blind to believe him. Jane and Ryan ate lunch together almost every day. Studying and eating in the cafeteria, heads close as they bent over a textbook, where everyone could see them. In fact, hadn't Brooke sat near them yesterday, just hours before Jane walked in on them in Ryan's bedroom?

"Brooke knew we were still together," Jane said, to no one in particular. "She knew and she didn't care."

As she heard the words echoing against the stark tiles and bare walls of the room, a new thought gripped her: maybe she could fix this? Maybe she could win Ryan back?

Jane turned to Ryan and laid a hand on his chest; he didn't flinch away but continued to breathe slowly, calmly. Receptively.

"I could quit my job," she said softly, her eyes pleading. "Tell my dad it's affecting my grades. Then I won't be so busy this summer. I'll be able to spend every free moment with you."

Ryan took a deep breath. Jane wasn't quite sure what that meant, but she decided to double down.

"I'll be an even better girlfriend. I'll be perfect. More perfect than Brooke. You'll love me if I'm perfect, right?"

Still not a word in response. Jane was beginning to feel desperate.

"What do you want me to do? Tell me, I'll do it. Anything." She grabbed the front of his shirt with both hands, balling the soft cotton jersey up in her fists, and buried her head in his chest. "I'll be whatever you want me to be, just don't leave me."

She waited several seconds, her forehead rising and falling against Ryan's chest, his breaths coming faster than before. She glanced up at his face, hoping to see him smiling back at her, signaling that he still loved her and would be with her forever. But his lips, though parted, certainly possessed no hint of a smile. If anything, they looked grimly resolute. And his eyes were no longer fixed on her. Instead, they focused over her shoulder. Jane turned, following his line of sight, and found herself staring directly into Brooke's eyes.

They were beautiful, Jane had to admit. A shade of greenish blue that she didn't even know existed in nature and which she would have attributed to colored contact lenses if she didn't know better. Their teal hue complemented Brooke's pale skin and blond hair to perfection, and Jane silently cursed her own genetic code that had given her mousey brown hair, limp and lifeless, boring brown eyes, and a dull skin tone that lacked Brooke's ethereal glow.

Jane sighed. She had forgotten Brooke was there, to be honest. She'd been so quiet in the corner of the room. Not moving. Not saying a word. Was she confused? Guilt-ridden? Biding her time until Jane's rant ended and she and Ryan could leave together?

Brooke was everything a guy like Ryan could want: gorgeous, sophisticated, popular. All the guys wanted to date her. All the girls wanted to be her. In comparison, Jane was a frumpy nobody. Literally plain Jane. Could she really blame Ryan for wanting to trade up?

Jane felt the tears welling up again and she turned away, unable to meet Brooke's gaze. The heavy droplets spilled over and down her cheeks in rapid succession, but her chest never heaved. The hysteria was gone and her anger, once ignited, had burned itself out, using up all the rage and jealousy and indignation that fueled it until only a smoldering heap remained.

And now, Jane was left with the sadness. Which was worse in so many ways. Her heart no longer felt as if someone had stabbed a dagger through it and was slowly, tortuously twisting the blade back and forth, churning Jane's organs to a pulp. Instead, there was a dull, ever-present ache in the recesses of her chest. And instead of hot tears and the overwhelming urge to scream obscenities at the top of her lungs, Jane could only whimper as the stark reality of a future without Ryan came crashing down on her.

Tomorrow at school, it would be Brooke eating lunch with Ryan in the cafeteria, Brooke giving him a good luck kiss before the next track meet, Brooke lying topless in Ryan's bed, door locked, skin touching.

And Jane would be alone.

She sniffled, rubbing the sleeve of her sweater across her nose, and felt something wet smear across her upper lip. She turned to the mirror, mounted on the arm of the dentist's chair, and noticed a streak of red on her face. Glancing down, Jane saw that the right sleeve of her sweater was utterly soaked in blood.

Right. She'd almost forgotten.

With a heavy sigh, Jane walked across the room and lifted a jar off the countertop. She held it up, examining the contents. "Brooke's eyes really are lovely," she said, smiling back at Ryan. "I can see why you wanted to be with her."

Jane turned to the figure slumped on the floor. A streak of blood trailed down the side of the wall, following the path of Brooke's descent after Jane had pulled her motionless body from the dentist's chair and flung her into the corner. Brooke hadn't moved in a while. How long had it been? Twenty minutes? An hour? She'd lost track of time while she'd wrestled Ryan's significantly heavier form, made even more cumbersome due to his lack of muscle control, into the chair Brooke had recently occupied. But surely the Novocain had worn off by now? Hard to say. Jane had used . . . a lot. Maybe too much. But what was done, was done.

Now it was Ryan's turn.

It had been so easy, once Jane had made her plan. A knock on Brooke's door, a quick jab of the needle to her neck near the spinal cord. She'd had the body in the trunk of her car before anyone had noticed. Ryan had been more of a challenge, but then, he never locked his car door, and so she waited for him after work, crouched low in the back seat of his car. He'd only seen her in the rear-view mirror when it was too late.

He was handsome even now, strapped into the dentist's chair, his face illuminated by harsh fluorescent bulbs. The skin of his forehead was turning bright red beneath the bungee cord secured tightly beneath the chair, and thick lines of drool snaked down from either corner of his gagged mouth. She'd heavily dosed Ryan with the local anesthetic but she didn't want him twitching during the procedure. That might ruin his perfectly handsome face.

Jane was very calm as she sat down in the stool and wheeled herself up beside him, just had she'd seen her dad do a million times before during exams. Her hands didn't tremble as she pressed the switch that tilted the chair back, dipping Ryan's head to waist level. There was even a smile on her face as she swung the tray of instruments toward her and selected a pair of dental forceps still caked in Brooke's coagulating blood.

She placed her hand lovingly on Ryan's forehead — it was hot and slick with sweat — and gazed down at him. "You won't feel a thing," she said, trying to sound soothing. After all, she was doing this for his own good. The eyes led the body. Remove the eyes, remove the temptation.

As Jane leaned over Ryan's face, forceps open, a comforting thought crossed her mind and she smiled.

My face will be the last thing he'll ever see.

Gretchen McNeil is the author of YA horror novels *Possess*, *Ten*, and 3:59, as well as the new mystery/suspense series Don't Get Mad, beginning in 2014 with *Get Even* and continuing in 2015 with *Get Dirty*, all with Balzer + Bray for HarperCollins. In 2016, Gretchen will publish two novels: *Relic*, a YA horror novel, and *I'm Not Your Manic Pixie Dream Girl*, her first YA contemporary. Gretchen also contributed an essay to the *Dear Teen Me* anthology from Zest Books.

Want more? Find a Q&A with Gretchen on page 242.

The One True Miranda Lieu

Kate Karyus Quinn

E VERYONE HAS THEIR BREAKING POINT. Turns out mine is having my father return from the dead.

I come home from school and there he is standing with Mother in the middle of the living room. His arm draped along her shoulders. Hers around his waist. They can't possibly be comfortable. It looks as if they're posing for a picture, and I can't help but wonder how long they've been waiting here. But then again they never do seem quite at ease when they're together.

"Miranda, isn't this a *surprise*?" my mother squeals, proving once again that she has mastered the art of the understatement. It's a shame they don't hand out trophies for that type of thing.

"I hate surprises," I answer. Which is true and which she would know if she paid the least bit of attention to me beyond what I'm wearing and how many times I've frowned ("Always aim for a zero frowny face day!").

My distrust of surprises goes all the way back to my fifth birthday party. It was on that bright and sunny day when I received a beautiful pink pony, her flowing mane braided and bowed. She was the most wonderful thing I'd ever seen and she was all mine to keep forever and always. In that first glimpse of her I imagined us having a million different adventures together. My love was instant and complete.

Still it was difficult to be gracious when my parents insisted my party guests be allowed to ride her before me. "After today she's all yours and only yours, Miranda," Father said with the same warm chuckle that always accompanied reprimands or admonishments to behave better. "Let the other children have a chance."

So I waited and waited until at last it was my turn. Of course, my parents had to make it a big production. As I approached the pony, a carrot clutched in my fist, all the other kids circled around, clapping and cheering. Just as I stretched out a hand to stroke her velvety soft nose, there was a terrible rumbling sound.

And then the beautiful pink pony spontaneously combusted.

So when someone mentions a surprise, perhaps it is inevitable that it always makes me think of being spattered with pink pony guts and the feel of them dripping off my face while all around me my friends screamed and screamed and screamed.

17

This then is why I don't rush to hug and kiss my long-lost father. One never knows who might blow up next.

Also, I rather hate him. I'd been told not to say such things when he was dead, but seeing as how he's miraculously resurrected, it looks like hating him is back on the table again.

Trust me, I have my reasons for it.

A year ago I caught him getting it on with Miss Gruber. Even naked I recognized her immediately. She'd been my teacher for kindergarten and then again in third grade. I'd had fond memories of her. She was always so encouraging. "Good job, sweetie," she'd say to everyone, even the kids who were doing a terrible job. With my father it was more of a "Yes, yes, just like that, sweetie baby," but the chirpy tone of encouragement was grossly familiar.

Really, it wasn't the cheating that had bothered me. I'd never believed my parents were in love or even particularly liked each other. But all that naked shaking flesh was unpleasant. Worse yet was my father announcing, "I'm sorry you walked in on me having relations with a woman who is clearly not your mother." Sometimes my father talked like he had a robot living inside him. Maybe that's why he's alive again.

Anyway, after he'd gotten dressed and sent Miss Gruber home we'd had a talk. He apologized and said he'd done things he wasn't proud of. A few tears had fallen (*his,* not mine; it's been years since I've given anyone the satisfaction of seeing me cry) and he'd quickly wiped them away. Then he asked if I was still his "little kitten?" I'd known the correct answer was, "Yes, of course." But honestly, had I ever been his little kitten? I had vague memories of him saying it once or twice when I was younger. Almost as if he was trying it out. But for him to bring it back after all this time . . .

"Kitten!" he exclaims now, apparently reading my mind, except not the part of it that thinks his nickname for me is gross and wrong.

"Surprise!" Mother says once more.

"I was never really dead," Father adds, that old chuckle bubbling up. "It was all just for the insurance money."

Mother glares at him like he's stepped on her lines. The moment feels familiar in a way that is neither warm nor comforting. She's always given him that same glare, as if every time he speaks he's stealing the words out of her mouth. Now she hisses, "Wait 'til she asks the question, *darling*."

I stare at my parents. These two strange slippery people that seem less knowable and more changeable the older I get. Oh I love them, of course. I suppose. But dear gods, I'd have given anything to know that I wouldn't have to share the same small town with them for the rest of my life.

We all stare at each other as the clock loudly ticks the seconds. None of us spontaneously combust. I try not to be disappointed.

19

"How about a hug for your old dad?" Father finally says after Mother gives him a sharp elbow in the ribs. "And then we can go to the Dairy Scoop for some ice cream. Just you and me, Kitten."

"Maybe another time." I answer. Then I politely nod at them and turn and walk up to my bedroom, firmly closing the door behind me.

I suppose they were expecting tears of joy and for me to throw myself into his arms. But too much has happened for that.

There was the cheating. Yes. That was awkward. But what came after was worse.

My mother went after him with a shotgun. She sprayed the dining room wall with shot and managed to get some in Father's left leg too. He lived. She went to jail. But then got off a week later. The judge said she'd had a temporary nervous breakdown and made her promise to never do it again. He winked at me then, where I was standing beside Mother who was beaming and yes, it wasn't my imagination, flirting with him. "Keep an eye on your mother, Miranda. And try not to upset her. She's a bad shot, but now that she's had some practice, who knows that she won't improve." Then he and Mother laughed and laughed and laughed.

Nobody ever mentioned it, but sometimes I wondered if the dirty bomb that kept our entire town under quarantine hadn't possibly also led to some brain disorders.

Anyway, my parents reconciled. It was lovely, I suppose, at least everyone said so, or it was until my father killed himself.

And tried to kill my mother too. Not with a shotgun, but poison. One second we were eating dinner and Mother was saying for the fifth time how much she loved this Ezonocore Nearly Chicken Pot Pie. She did that a lot. Got hooked on how great some new thing she'd bought was and couldn't stop repeating it over and over and over again. Also, the pot pie was terrible. I was shoving a pile of it around my plate when Mother and then Father fell from their chairs and began convulsing on the kitchen floor. Then foam started dribbling out from between their lips.

Later, after Father was dead and buried and Mother had recovered, they told us it was poison and that Father had been behind all of it.

"Things will get better," Mother kept saying, but they never did. Not really. Or not long enough for one to feel safe, as if the worst was really and truly over.

And now this.

It doesn't feel better. It feels worse. And unsettling in the worst sort of way.

Unable to sleep, I pull back the curtains and seek out my old friend Vega, the fifth brightest star in the night sky. I'm not quite sure when or why I decided to fixate on the fifth brightest star, rather than the very shiniest one in the galaxy; it was such a long time ago that my reasons are forgotten and don't matter much anymore.

At this point, even if Vega was the least brightest star, she would still be my favorite.

But tonight something is wrong with her. She blinks. Off. On. Off. On. Off. And then steadily back on once more, returning to normal.

It's subtle, but eventually I count it out and realize the little stutter of light is happening every forty-seven seconds.

I scan the horizon. The neat rows of houses. The silhouette of the bicycle horn factory at the far end of town. And the water tower at the center of Rockwell Falls, stretching so high that it almost seems as if one could stand upon it and touch the stars.

It's a fanciful thought, the sort I've learned to keep to myself. And yet for some reason, I decide to test it out anyway.

I sail down the stairs and then out the front door. Skipping, I jump right over the steps that lead down from the porch and onto the green expanse of our lawn.

Then I begin to run.

I've always loved running. Even though there is nowhere to go, it is the only way I know to get rid of the nervous energy that constantly fills me. Terrible things occur regularly. And as awful as they are it's the waiting between them that bothers me most. The wondering of what will be next.

Now, I don't pace myself. Leaning into the windless night (they are all windless nights, I can't help reflecting), I push harder than I ever have before, until it feels like I am running *from* instead of *to* something.

And perhaps I am. I honestly don't know anymore. In this instant, there is only running and confusion. Then, too soon, the water tower looms before me.

The ladder is far beyond the reach of my fingertips. Yet allowing defeat does not occur to me. Grabbing a chair from the café around the corner, I climb on it and then with a little jump manage to grab hold. Pretending it's the monkey bars at the playground, I slowly, achingly pull myself—

A bright light hits me. I freeze. Then the unmistakable sound of Sheriff Alfie Arnold's voice amplified through his car speaker blasts out. "Miranda Lieu. You are trespassing on private property. Come down at once."

It's impossible to see beyond the glare of the light, but I know the Sheriff well enough to clearly picture him. Tall, thin, and almost comically gangly, when Sheriff Alfie is being serious he tends to put his hands on his hips and puff out his concave chest. Mostly, though, the Sheriff isn't at all interested in being serious. He's known for having specially modified the trunk of his cop cruiser so that it's refrigerated and can carry all different types of frozen treats. With crime almost non-existent, Sheriff Alfie is more ice cream man than sheriff. And to fill out the rest of his time, he plays the role of clown. He's famous for his pratfalls down staircases, usually involving multiple somersaults before he reaches the bottom. It's also common to find headlines in the weekly newspaper that read, "SHERIFF LOCKS HIMSELF IN CELL AGAIN: Blames Sticky Bolt."

So after the surprise of being caught passes, I have no hesitation in yelling back at Alfie, "I'll be down in a minute! I just need to check something first!" and then continue climbing.

With hands and feet on the ladder, I make good time and nearly reach the top when another voice shouts up at me. "Miranda, this is Pastor Karen. Come on, Hon, you've been through a lot, but you and I and all the Gods know, this is not the answer."

Pastor Karen, usually so calm and soothing, sounds shaken. I pause again.

It occurs to me that I've been found out very quickly. And that all these people have arrived amazingly fast. Also that they seem to believe I'm planning something drastic.

Maybe I am. I don't know yet. I gotta get up there first.

I reach for the next rung—and then I am at the top where the ladder curves, taking me all the way to the water tower's roof that slopes gently upwards, like the stomach of a sleeping giant after a large meal.

"Miranda!" The third voice to shout at me is from Mother. As I already suspected this was coming, I barely listen as she demands, "Miranda Lieu, get back down here this instant."

Instead I turn my face up toward the sky. It's so close. Although I'd been trying to reach it, I can't help but feel as if it snuck up on me. And yet somehow it's smaller too. A few steps take me to the peak of the roof, bringing me that much closer to the stars. Raising both arms over my head, I watch my fingers unfurl like flowers blooming, lifting their heads to the sun.

And then to my surprise the glow of the stars illuminates each one of my fingertips. No, it's more than just their reflected light, the stars are in the palms of my hands. And when I try to capture them in my fists, they end up on the backs of my knuckles instead.

The stars are nothing but an elaborate light show.

The realization comes, hard and irrefutable. One terrible truth, followed quickly by a multitude of questions.

Is the lie what I'd read in books about stars being balls of gas millions of miles away? Or is this pale light the lie? Are all the rules of the universe just stories we've been told to keep things orderly?

A growing number of voices swell from below and there is the clank of someone rapidly climbing up the ladder toward me.

I ignore all that and instead turn my attention to the town spread out before me. Rockwell Falls like I've never seen it before. When I'd looked out from my window, I'd noticed the houses and the neat yards around them. Now I can see all of it. The school. The town square, with four perfect corners exactly as advertised. None of this particularly interests me, though. Even from a new angle it is just the same as it's always been. Then my gaze drifts to the edge of town. I have found the limits of the sky, perhaps there are natural ends here too.

There is the bicycle factory whose smokestacks even at this late hour belch out white clouds that keep the whole western end of town in a permanent fog. Running alongside the factory is the old cemetery, inhabited by restless spirits strong enough to do harm to flesh and blood. No one in their right mind ventures there. Next come the woods with trees packed so tightly together it's nearly impossible to squeeze between them. And finally, the caverns round out the final border of my tiny town.

I've taken it all for granted. Assumed this is simply the way of life here in Rockwell Falls. Never did I ever think that it might be all made up.

There were even history and science lessons about it at school, complete with pop quizzes and the story of a brave girl named Molly who'd lived through the terrible war that led to the dirty bomb getting dropped on our town.

The crazy thing about the bomb is we'd known it was coming. But instead of evacuating and tipping off the enemy, we'd bravely stayed put with only an energy net surrounding Rockwell Springs. In theory, metal poles set up all over town would send out signals creating an energy field capable of capturing and holding the nuclear radiation the bomb was meant to spread. Amazingly, it worked. Everyone survived. The only problem was that afterwards no one could leave or enter Rockwell Springs without disturbing the energy field and with it the radiation held high above the clouds. Invisible but always there overhead.

That was all before I was born, but even now we all know the only things that keep the sky from falling are the steel beams they pounded into the ground and stretched up into the sky, spacing them at even intervals from one end of town to the other. We try not to dwell on the whole being trapped thing, though. Instead every year we celebrate the courage of Rockwell Falls on the day the bomb was dropped. Book reports, dioramas, and historical reenactments have all hammered the point home again and again.

There was never any reason to doubt.

Now though it looks false. Obviously, nearly blindingly so. This is not a sky above me, fallen or otherwise. It's an optical illusion. A trick of light.

A new thought comes then. Along with it a sense of sureness. Of inevitability.

It stalls as someone grabs hold of my hand. Pastor Karen stands there with her kindly but firm smile. "Come child," she says, giving our connected hands a small insistent tug. "Be reasonable."

It's the worst thing she could have said. Almost as bad as *surprise*.

You see, after the pink pony incident, I was different. Jumpy. Given to tears at any small noise. And I resolutely refused to wear any of the pink outfits filling my closet.

Overnight I'd decided my new favorite color was black. That's when Father told me about the ghoul that came to take unhappy little girls away. He and Mother gave me some happy pills to help me smile so that the ghoul wouldn't want me. The pills made me laugh when nothing was the slightest bit funny. They made me skip because it itched to stand still. They made me seem very much like a happy little girl, while inside I was watching my pony explode on an endless loop. But time passed and no ghoul came and so it seemed like a fair trade.

Eventually I stopped taking the pills, except for after certain incidents when I'd get shaky again and they'd begin showing up next to my morning glass of orange juice once more. Then when I was twelve, Grandma died. Amazingly, she'd passed away quietly in her own bed after being sick for several months. There was nothing surprising about it at all. And yet I was devastated. It was so much worse than losing the pink pony. When the pills returned once more, I ignored them.

"Miranda dear," Father chuckled genially while tapping his finger on the table to call my attention to the pill sitting there. "Don't forget about the ghoul. Do you want him to get you?" I stared at Father and Mother smiling encouragingly beside him.

Instead of picking up my pill, I reached for the bat that I'd used yesterday at softball practice. I brought it down onto the table, smashing the pill into powder. Then I grinned at my parents, without the aid of any pill. "Let him try."

Which is to say, there are times when one just cannot be reasonable.

I jerk my hand free of Pastor Karen's. And without another word, I take two leaps toward the edge of the water tower—

And jump.

Everything is a lie. My knees bend and I push against the solid surface beneath me, launching into the air, giving myself the closest thing I can to my long held and despaired of dream that I might one day go up into space and explore the stars.

And if everything is a lie, if up is down and down is up and real is false, well then perhaps I won't fall. Maybe I will fly. And then I will finally truly live, instead of being smashed to bits like a happy pill going up against a wooden bat.

Except, of course, I fall.

The equivalent of five stories go by quickly, but still there is time enough for the panic, the uncertainty to all fade away.

Do I want to die?

No, I want the exact opposite. What I want, with an all too real desperation, is escape. And choices. And so I leapt.

Even as my death rushes toward me I cannot regret it. And I still hope, hope for—

I hit the ground. It hurts. It—

* * *

"What fresh hell is this?"

Those were my grandmother's last words. I'm pretty sure it wasn't an indication of where she was headed afterlife-wise since it was a phrase she pulled out quite regularly.

After she died, I sorta adopted it as my own. Sometimes I'd use it to start the day, my own little variation on the more prosaic "good morning."

So when I wake with a feeling that something is wrong—or maybe I should say, more wrong than usual—I of course wonder, *What fresh hell is this?*

The first problem is the tube coming out of my nose and wrapped around my head. Then there's the needle jutting from the back of my hand, with another tube running out of it. And finally, suction cups on nearly every inch of me spitting out wires that then connect me to the giant machines circling my bed.

I try to sit up, but my whole body, stiff and strange, fights every movement. It takes me three tries to make my arm swing upwards and several negotiations before my fingers agree to cooperate and curl around the thing in my nose so that I can pull it away.

I close my eyes then. Exhausted. Yet wide awake all at the same time.

It is then that I notice the quiet. No crickets chirping in the grass. No birds tweeting on my window ledge. No soft murmur of my parents' voices downstairs. It is a silence so vast and unknown that it makes my chest ache with a rather extreme version of what I usually only think of as "loneliness."

What happened? I wonder. But then, of course, I remember. A false sky. The world rushing past me. The ground rising up to meet me.

Dying.

I am almost certain I remember dying.

And yet. Here I am. My room transformed into a hospital. My body in one piece.

Testing that theory, I slowly inch upwards in bed and then wiggle my toes and flex my feet and shake my legs out, until my whole body feels a little more lived in. And a little more my own.

Getting up on my feet takes a few tries, but once I manage to get fully upright I find that I can shuffle along okay. Slowly, I make my way to the bathroom and after emptying my bladder, I study my face in the mirror. It looks the same. Almost as if I'd never experienced a high impact collision with concrete. I pull my lips back, baring my teeth. They're all present and accounted for.

Finally I look down at my hands, the same ones that had touched the stars. The fake stars. In a fake sky. In a fake town.

So why should I be surprised that I'm alive? If everything is fake, why shouldn't I be as well?

Shaking my head at the strangeness of all this, I walk out my bedroom door and then down the hallway; hitting the creaking floorboard, I pick up speed. The stairs are under my feet and at the bottom of them I half expect to see Mother and Father . . . but instead there is only the living room furniture draped in white sheets and a house with a sort of shut-in feeling. I don't know what to make of it all, so I just keep putting one foot in front of another.

I hesitate at the front door, the knob cool in my hand. It seems bigger than simply exiting the house, even though I'm not sure exactly how or why. Pulling the door open, I travel the same path I did only . . . was it yesterday? Across the porch, down the steps, onto the wide green lawn, that looks sadly brown at the moment . . .

I stop, planting my feet.

The light is strange. Flat. Neither day nor night. And the whole town is so empty and silent, except for a distant faint buzzing sound, but otherwise the quiet stretches in all directions. Tilting my head back to look up into the sky, my first thought when I see what's above is annihilation.

This is why it's so silent. That false sky has finally fallen and taken everyone with it. There is no sun. No moon. Instead row after row of flickering fluorescent lights have replaced them and given the whole town a sickly glow.

"Don't panic," comes a voice from beside me. "Nothing terrible has happened."

I look over. It's a man, all in black including the hood covering his entire head.

"Are you the ghoul that carries away unhappy girls?" I ask. I ought to be afraid, I suppose, but he looks so foolish that it's rather difficult to take him seriously. Also, I am rarely afraid mid-crisis. It's only when it's over that I tend to fall apart.

"I'm a friend," he answers in the serious sort of tone that doesn't match his silly disguise. "One of many," he adds. "We're getting you out of here."

"Oh? Out of where exactly? Are we in hell then? That would explain a lot."

"No, of course not," the man responds, sounding appalled. "You're not dead. Technically, you were unresponsive for a few hours, but that's nothing. Revival medicine is advanced enough that so long as tissue samples and blood have been regularly harvested—" He stops, gives himself a shake. "We really don't have time to get into this."

The talk of my being dead and then revived has shaken me a bit, I admit, but I smile at him blandly. "We don't? Why not?"

"Because we're leaving," he answers as if this should be obvious. And this time he clarifies, "We're leaving Rockwell Falls."

"Where are we going?" I ask, but then before he can answer, I throw out another question, one I'm pretty sure I've already answered. But a second opinion never hurts. "It's all fake then, isn't it?" I spread my arms out as if embracing all of it, and then I let them fall, throwing it away. "I saw the stars. I saw them and I knew, but the thing I really want to know is . . ." I pause and swallow, needing a moment to find the right words.

"The rest of the world, whatever there is of it, it's real, isn't it? I mean it can't all just be made up."

"Oh yes. It's real," the man says, somewhat caustically as if this isn't a point in its favor. Then perhaps remembering that he's supposed to be selling me on that other world, he adds, "It's at least bigger than what you got here. Would you like to see it?"

Would I like to see it?

I look around Rockwell Falls once more, realizing at last what it always has been—a gigantic playset no different than the dollhouse I used to have in my bedroom. "Did everyone leave because they found out? Is that what happened?" Another thought occurs to me. "Grandma told me that our family had lived in Rockwell Falls for generations. How long has this been going on? Do Mother and Father know? The Mayor? Pastor Karen?"

The more the questions come, the more the man in black shifts his feet and seems in general rather uncomfortable. "I'd rather not get into it, but if you insist . . . "

"I do insist."

He sighs. "Everyone knew. Everyone except you. This whole place was built just for you."

"For me?" I can't help but laugh at the very idea. "But why me?"

"Well, that's complicated. There's a story that was told and then the truth behind it. I can't get into right now. You'd have to understand the politics and intergalactic space travel—"

I laugh again, not caring that I sound half hysterical. "Intergalactic space travel?"

"Never mind that." He stops and looks around, almost nervously. "We really can't keep standing here chatting. Do you want to leave or not?"

"All I've ever wanted is to leave here." It's not precisely true. Once all I ever wanted was a pink pony with a braided mane. And despite how poorly that turned out, and despite how my heart races and how I can think of at least twenty different ways *this* could blow up in my face, I am determined to go anyway.

And so we leave.

Amazing all the old memories that come up as we walk through town. Things I haven't thought about in a long time. There is the spot where at seven years of age I attended my first and last Lady Scouts meeting. It hit a small snag when our bonfire suddenly raged out of control, inexplicably surrounding us. As we huddled together the Scout Leader instructed us to "Die bravely." Luckily, the fire truck arrived before we had to prove our courage.

We pass by the bicycle horn factory which we visited for my fifth grade field trip. Every child was given a bicycle horn fresh off the assembly line and it was great fun until a scream sounded high and hysterical above the hum and groan of the machinery. Joanna Livingston lost her arm to a machine that . . . Well no one was ever really clear on exactly *what* the machine did. What I do remember with perfect clarity, though, was the blood and

Joanna's severed arm traveling along a conveyor belt in an endless circle around us, over and over again, almost as if it were on display while all of the children screamed.

The hooded man pauses as we reach the graveyard. Or perhaps I am the one who brings us to a stop. Most people are afraid of the cemetery. Ghost sightings are common and everyone knows that venturing into the woods beyond the last row of graves will cause a great snarling pack of wolves to come flying out and tear you limb from limb. I'd seen it happen to Jimmy Monroe. He was never the same after that. I suppose none of us were.

But after Grandma died I'd conquered my fear to visit her grave every single week. I walk straight to it now, noting that there is no trace of the flowers I left last time. Kneeling before it, I place a hand on the familiar grave marker. From the corner of my eye, I can see the man in black standing a few steps way, clearly not wanting to intrude. "Is she even buried here?" I ask. And then an even more incredible thought occurs to me. "Is she even dead?"

"Yes, she's dead, I'm sorry." He shuffles forward, but I don't look up at him. "But no, I don't think she's buried here. She well . . ."

"It's all fake," I say, trying to remind myself of this simple fact, even while I can't quite understand it. Something in me breaks then.

Abruptly, I stand and race through the rest of the graveyard. I don't stop at the tree line, but step right into them until they surround me on all sides, the branches

KATE KARYUS QUINN

snatching at my clothing. Even as my shirt rips, I keep going, feeling sick to my stomach at being in this forbidden spot, despite reminding myself it is all nonsense. And then suddenly the trees end and a wall that stretches all the way up into the sky stands before me.

I watch as the man in black reaches toward the wall and suddenly a door opens in it, silently sliding upwards, revealing a whole new world beyond Rockwell Falls. He walks through the doorway, casually, as if this moment wasn't the slightly bit momentous. After a few seconds of hesitation, I follow.

Inside the room I count twenty television screens. They line a full wall, one stacked upon another. And each shows a different part of Rockwell Falls. The school. The park. The ice cream parlor. And my bedroom. Ten of them show my bedroom from various angles. One looks straight down at my empty bed.

And finally, I get it.

All those things hadn't been to fool everyone.

It had all been for a single person.

Me.

"They've been watching me. That's what the whole town is for. And everyone else knew because they were . . . pretending. Like people on stage in a play."

The man says nothing in response. He just looks at me, sadly. Well perhaps not sadly. It is hard to tell with his face covered, but I can sense a certain air of pity wafting from him.

37

Beneath the television screens is a long panel of buttons and knobs and little slider things. One of them is labeled "Dead Grandma," and I can't resist pushing it, half believing my grandma will materialize before me. Instead, I hear her humming. It's barely musical. Just a collection of hm, hm, hm noises going up and down. She did this while cleaning or thinking about something tricky. And then, of course, after she died, I'd heard it sometimes when visiting her grave. It never failed to send a shiver down my spine.

"They—" the man starts to say, but I hold up a hand, not wanting to hear it. I understand what they did without him having to explain it. They took the sound of her humming and fed it to me so they could watch me water her fake grave with my very real tears. The only time I cried, thinking I was safely alone.

But I was never ever alone.

Suddenly a thousand embarrassing and supposedly private scenes flash before my eyes. "Did they watch me in the bathroom? When I got changed? In the shower?" I demand.

"No, no," he says, and just as I relax a bit, he adds, "I mean not unless you paid extra. And even then it's only a few flashes of skin, hardly worth the . . ."

"AUUGHGHGHHH!" I scream before he can say anything else.

It doesn't really help, though. I've already heard too much.

I take a step, blindly, my head spinning. Disaster has been a part of my life since as long as I can remember. Between catastrophes I'd begin to quiver in anticipation of the next one. By the time it actually struck, all I felt was relief. I have become very good at damage control. After every disaster, I was able to mostly pull it together. Or fake it until I couldn't anymore. But this, this is beyond my coping abilities.

The man's hands settle on my shoulders and turn me from television screens that have stolen my life and given it away. I let him, not fighting as he propels me forward, until we enter an elevator. Distantly I note that it's quite a bit more rounded and sleek than the one in the court building at the center of town. Then the door shushes shut behind us and we are hurtling upwards. My ears pop several times and yet we keep going up, up, up until finally with a jolt we abruptly stop. The doors part and the man leads me out into a small echoing room. Deserted. Like everything else.

Even though I'm getting a bit tired of him pushing me around, I allow it until we step outside the building into the darkness of night that I somehow immediately recognize as being different. As being real.

The first clue is that the air stinks of rot and death, and the very act of breathing causes us to gasp and gag and shudder and retch. I clench my stinging eyes shut against it as I fall to my knees. Something soft presses against my face.

"Scented handkerchief," the man tells me. When I breathe in again, the stench is filtered through a floral type of perfume. "They built Rockwell Falls beneath the South central landfill, sorta as a way to disguise it. And discourage people from investigating too."

"We were underground," I say to the man, already knowing it's true. "The whole time, we've been buried."

"Yep," he confirms.

"And is this it? Right here? Is this all that's left of the world beside Rockwell Falls?"

"Oh no," he quickly replies. "This is only a tiny bit of it that everyone else has left behind." He gestures to the towering mountains surrounding us on all sides. "Soon the sun will rise and you'll see they're made of piles of trash. You'll be long gone by then, though. We just need to wait here. Your ride should be along any second now."

I have a hundred other questions, but as I tip my head back, every one of them falls away, lost to the enormous expanse of the night sky towering above me.

It's nearly impossible to take in the size and breadth of this sky and the stars spread across it.

Oh the stars!

I breathe and then exhale, hyperventilating and not caring or even noticing the fetid air, too overcome with the wonder of stars.

The stars I'd known before were dim bulbs and uniform lights compared to these, some of which are like diamond chunks of light while others are handfuls of silvery golden glitter scattered across the sky. The stars in Rockwell Falls are like everything in that town, always threatening to fall, while these are so far away and so brilliant and so uncountable, just looking at them makes me feel small and insignificant and yet part of something larger, something—

I stretch out my hands and don't come close to catching them. No water tower would be high enough for me to get even the tips of fingers within reach of them.

Tears fill my eyes, putting the sky underwater, and then I gaze at it that way.

Of course, it's more than just stars, more than just sky. It's the whole world being cracked wide open and spilling out everywhere.

I am searching the sky for Vega when I spot something that isn't a star. It isn't anything that I have any context for at all. "What is that?" I ask the man, my finger pointing the way toward the tiny squares of light up among the stars.

"Oh that," he says, like someone who finds a topic not particularly interesting. "It's one of the big ships they're filling up with people and sending off into the universe. Pilgrims, you know? They believe they can find a new earth out there."

"I want to go with them," I say, without having to think about it first.

He laughs at me. Not meanly. But not in a very nice way either. "Up here isn't like that candy colored world you lived in down there. Hardly nothing's fair or soft or pretty. And it doesn't all revolve around you. Why do you think everyone wants to get off this place and take their chances on something that might not even be out there? But to get a ride on a ship you gotta be essential personnel. Doctors, scientists, those types. Or a politician. And you're . . . well you're Miranda Lieu, or you were, but you won't be anymore. Once we get you away from here we'll have to keep you hidden for a bit. And then change your name . . . maybe even your face." He stops saying these terrible distressing things, not because he sees that I don't like them, but because a car pulls up in front of us.

The vehicle is nothing like the ones in Rockwell Falls. Those are boats on wheels with huge fins and ornate grills, while this is sleek and small. The doors flip upward and then a girl steps out.

I thought we'd reached the quota on surprises, but that was clearly a mistake.

Because astonishingly, this girl looks exactly like me. Same height. Same nose. Same smile, although hers is friendlier than any I've worn recently.

She puts a hand out, "Miranda, oh my goodness. I'm a big fan. And it's such an honor to help you out."

I don't take her hand. "Should I know you?"

She laughs, in an uncertain sort of way. "No. I'm . . . "

As she trails off, the man in black fills in. "She's a look-alike. Lots of 'em out there. Some for fun. Some for work. There are doctors who specialize in reconstructive surgery. They run ads on the feeds for your show. Book Dr. Stew and you too—"

" — can look like Miranda Lieu." He and the girl say it together in this sing-songy kind of way.

I stare at him, wishing I could see his face. He sounds so matter of fact about the whole thing. So just to clarify, I ask, "Doctors who specialize in making people look like me?"

The girl answers with an eager smile. "Dr. Stew has the catchiest jingle, but Dr. Vinshu is the best. She did my facial structure."

"Uh-huh," I say, because really? But then again, the man in black mentioned me needing a new face so maybe I'll be visiting Dr. Vinshu soon. The thought sends a ripple of alarm through me. "And why are you here?"

With that the girl looks uncertain again. Again she turns to the man in black who takes hold of my arm. "We really need to go."

I jerk away from him, suddenly not seeing him as quite so harmless. "Why is she here?" I demand.

He sighs. "A decoy. We put her in your bed. They'll figure out pretty quickly it's not you, but it'll buy us some time."

"But," I stare at the girl who looks so amazingly like me, she might be my mirror reflection. "Why would they come after me? Why wouldn't they just keep her?"

The girl looks at me as if I'm insane. "Keep me? But *you're* the one true Miranda Lieu. They couldn't, they wouldn't — " she trails off, apparently so shocked at the very idea that words fail her.

The man in black steps in to explain once more. "The One True Miranda Lieu's the name of the show. It's your brand. Why do you think they spent so much putting you back together? They can't put in a decoy. If it got found out . . . the point of the show is that it's you."

That's when I finally get it. This is a prison break. And they—whoever set up that fake town down there—will be coming after me. Which means that I'll be running and hiding for the rest of my life. I wonder if even a new face will be enough to keep me concealed.

Sorta makes my escape seem less freeing. I look up at the stars again and they are farther away than ever. Then I close my eyes and remember plummeting from the water tower.

Sometimes you have to die to live.

Sometimes you have to go down to go up . . . especially if want to go all the way up to the stars.

Decision made, I turn to the man in black. "Take me back."

He argues with me then. Tells me how for years the "Free Miranda Lieu" movement has grown and when I jumped from the water tower they saw it as a cry for help. When they found out I was still alive, they decided to get me out of there once and for all. Then he gets into logistics. How many people were needed to make this happen, how they shut off the power for Rockwell Falls, how this is the only chance because tomorrow everyone returns and filming starts again . . .

I am only half-listening, but that last part catches my attention. "Everyone comes back tomorrow?" I ask to make sure I heard him right.

"Yeah, that's what I just said."

"Well, I can't leave without saying good-bye, can I?"

Actually, he feels that this is the only way to leave. I continue to disagree until at last he capitulates. Although, not graciously. Not hiding his frustration, he puts the girl, who looks like me but isn't me, back in the quiet little car which then goes purring away. For her part, she appears to be mostly confused by the whole thing, but at least she doesn't try to argue. And finally, while he mutters beneath his breath the entire way, we ride down the elevator and from there he tells me in this snide tone to find my own home.

So I do.

Actually, I prefer not having him by my side as I stroll through town for the second time that night, seeing it with new eyes. Or newer eyes. Suddenly seeing all of its possibilities.

All those terrible things that happened here hadn't been natural disasters.

Each and every one had been manufactured to get a reaction.

Out of me.

And everyone had known.

Except me.

After taking the long way around town, I am thoroughly exhausted by all my adventures. Back home, I climb into bed and snuggle beneath my covers. Settling my head on my pillow, I feel calm in a way I've never experienced before. The constant tension of waiting for the next terrible thing to happen is gone. Not because there won't be anymore awful shocking incidents.

But because this time I'll be the one behind them.

As I close my eyes I can't help but imagine my mother waking me up tomorrow. She'll pull back the covers and see a product not much different than an Ezonocore Nearly Chicken Pot Pie. For her the one true Miranda Lieu is just something else to sell.

And beyond her those concealed cameras connected to who knows how many watching eyes, some of them no doubt wondering why I didn't escape when I had the chance. Others simply cheering for the next disaster.

I'll gaze back at all of them, docile and sweet.

Like a beautiful pink birthday pony.

With a terrible surprise hidden inside.

Kate Karyus Quinn is an avid reader and menthol chapstick addict. She has lived in California and Tennessee, but recently made the move back to her hometown of Buffalo, New York, with her husband and two children in tow. She promised them wonderful people, amazing food, and weather that would . . . build character. She is the author of *Another Little Piece, (Don't You) Forget About Me,* and the upcoming *Down With The Shine* all from HarperTeen.

Want more? Find a Q&A with Kate on page 244.

Such a Lovely Monster

Justina Ireland

I HAVE A MONSTER UNDER MY BED.

He's always been there, as long as I can remember. When I was a little kid I'd wake in the middle of the night and see odd shadows dancing on the wall, a sure sign of some otherworldly creature in my room. I would clutch my covers to my chest and scream out for my mom, huddling on my bed like it was an island of safety. She would come running down the hall, eyes bleary, hair wrapped up in a brightly colored scarf for the night.

"Damn, girl, what's your problem?" she'd ask, standing in the doorway, yawning widely.

"There's a monster under my bed," I'd whisper, staring at the edge of my mattress, waiting for a scaled hand to reach up for me at any moment.

"Well, stay in bed. He can't get you as long as you stay in your bed," she'd answer. Which, in hindsight, was not the most encouraging thing to say.

"Now go back to sleep. I don't want to hear anymore nonsense." Then my momma would go back to bed, the light from the hallway filtering into my room and casting shadows that looked like grasping hands and malevolent, hulking figures.

I would stay up all night, senses on high alert, convinced that at any moment the monster under my bed would come slinking out and I would be eaten in a single gulp. Exhaustion would eventually overwhelm me, and I'd finally fall asleep sometime before dawn. It happened like that for a week before my mom intervened.

"Tamara, listen," she said one morning as I ate my Lucky Charms. "There *is* a monster under your bed. Everyone needs a place to live, even monsters. That monster has lived in this house since it was built, and he was part of us being able to move here. How else do you think we could afford such a nice area?"

It was true. The last place we lived was a cramped apartment where we could hear the neighbors fight until all hours of the night. Sometimes you could hear the sharp pop-pop-pop of gunfire as the local boys fought out in the streets. The walls of the apartment building were covered in graffiti, and chip bags and soda cans littered the gutters like fallen leaves.

Our new neighborhood was nothing like that. At night the only thing you could hear were crickets chirping out a melody and the soft sighs of the house settling in for the evening. Outside there was a yard where I could run and jump as much as I wanted and even a tire swing hanging from a big old tree. There were kids in the neighborhood who played games of tag in the street, and even though I wasn't yet allowed to leave the yard I'd sometimes sneak out and join them. This house was a much better place than our last home.

"But, can't you switch rooms with me?" I asked.

Mom shook her head. "Doesn't work that way. No matter where you go that monster would just follow. He's your monster, now. He picked you. All you can do is make the most of it."

So, I did.

I began to give myself rules for dealing with the monster under my bed. I couldn't get out of bed without turning on the light. Turning on my bedside lamp was how the monster knew I was just going to the bathroom in the middle of the night. And even then, I couldn't just climb out of bed like a normal person. I had to jump from my bed to the middle of the room, and sometimes if I didn't jump far enough I could feel the monster reaching for me, grasping fingers and ill intent.

I made sure that I never slept with my hand hanging over the side of the bed. Because the monster would eat me. A couple of times I woke to the monster licking my palm in a way that was gross and more than just a little terrifying. After that, I learned to sleep pressed up against the wall.

I couldn't have pets.

For my tenth birthday my mom got me a kitten. "Make sure he stays out of your room," she said as she handed me the squirming ball of gray fur. "You'll have to keep your door closed. Promise me you'll keep your door closed so he doesn't go into your room."

"I promise," I said.

But I was only a kid, and I wasn't as careful as I should've been. I left for school one day, rushing out to catch the bus. When I came home my bedroom door was open just the tiniest crack and there was a single tuft of hair on the floor of my room. Nothing else.

That was the last time I saw Stormy.

After my kitten disappeared, Mom got kind of worried. I dunno, maybe she only half believed in the monster under my bed. Maybe she thought that I was just a kid who overreacted and that our landlord, Mr. Klein, was just some old kooky white dude. After all, he was the one who warned Mom about the monster before we even rented the place. But after Stormy, Mom became a little crazy.

"Here," she'd say, forcing a plate at me. "Put this next to your bed." From then on I would take a plate of leftovers and put it beside my bed every night before I went to sleep. In the morning, the plate was clean. It was a small price to pay to guarantee the monster didn't eat me, but I was never really sure I was safe. Even though I'd come to think of the monster as my monster I was pretty certain he'd eat me just as soon as he got the chance.

I couldn't tell any of my friends at school about the monster. They would've thought I was crazy. That's what Mom said.

"I know it's hard, baby, especially now when everyone is hanging out with each other and doing sleepovers, but you can't have anyone over to the house. We just don't know what the monster will do." When she said it her expression grew shadowed. I didn't know if she was remembering Stormy's unfortunate fate or imagining something terrible happening to me. Either way, no sleepovers. It was a house rule.

And I couldn't even have people over. Somehow, the monster knew when strangers were near. When my Aunt Cecelia came to visit from Baltimore I woke to her standing in the doorway to my room.

"You hear that, TamTam?" she asked, voice dreamy. "There's singing. The prettiest singing I've ever heard."

"What singing?" I asked Aunt Cecelia, but she just closed her eyes and swayed.

"Oh, that choir, those sounds. Like heaven in my ears."

"MOM!" I yelled, my voice shrill.

She'd appeared and had escorted Aunt Cecelia back to the couch in the living room. That was the last time family came up to visit.

That was the last time anyone came to visit.

"It's the monster," Mr. Klein, our landlord, explained when Mom brought it up the next time he came over. "Generally it won't touch thems that's residents, but strangers is fair game. You're better off not having people over."

"We can't live here anymore," Mom said, her gaze flicking from me to the door. "This is just insane."

"I'll take another $100 off your rent," Mr. Klein said. "I never had no one stay as long as you folks."

So we stayed, and Mom bought a new TV and a computer for my room.

"It's not that bad," she said. I think she half believed it.

"We should do a sleepover at your house, Tam." My best friend Rai was always hinting that we should hang out at my house. She had a thing for a boy in my neighborhood, Tyler Soren, so the more time she could spend at my house, the better. I'd spent the night over at her place a couple of times, but I never returned the invitation. It made me seem like an asshole, but I couldn't break Mom's No Sleepovers rule. Not even for Rai.

This was a problem. The entirety of our eighth grade year, Rai's world revolved around Tyler, who was pretty much an uncaring sun. A million sleepovers at my house wouldn't alert Tyler to Rai's existence, but it's not like I could tell her that.

"I can't have sleepovers," I said. That was it. No explanation, no apologies.

"Why don't you ask your mom? Have you even tried asking her?"

"No sleepovers."

During the summer between eighth and ninth grade I woke up to someone crawling in my window, which I'd left propped open to let in the breeze.

"Who's there?" I called.

"Relax, Tamara, it's just me. I was at Tyler's house. My parents think I'm spending the night here, though—" The rest of her words were cut off. There was a rustling noise and a wet gurgle.

And then, nothing.

The next morning there was a police officer at our door.

"Hi. I'm here to ask you a few questions about Rai Chakravarty."

"What happened?" Mom asked, not wasting any time.

"She's missing," the officer said. He was young, blond, and looked like he wanted to be anywhere but on our porch, asking us questions. "Her parents told us she was supposed to be spending the night here."

"Absolutely not. Tamara isn't allowed to have sleepovers. Rai wasn't here, was she?" Mom asked, her expression somewhere between fear and anger.

"No. No, I haven't seen her." The memory of that wet gurgling sound came back, a sound almost like something large swallowing. I forced the thought away.

"I haven't seen her since last week," I said.

They searched for Rai for three weeks before someone important decided that she was probably just another one of those unfortunate cases, sneaking around in the dark after hanging out with a boy, a tender morsel for a nightmare predator.

If only they knew how right that was.

Rai's parents held a funeral with an empty casket the first week of ninth grade. I didn't go.

It felt wrong.

Instead, I pushed all of my fear and sadness down deep and pretended like it didn't hurt, like I wasn't crushed at the thought that somehow, it was my fault that my best friend was dead. If only I'd told her about the monster under my bed she would still be alive.

If only.

I entered high school with a new group of friends. But not really friends. Just people I knew. I wasn't allowed to have friends after letting my last one get eaten by the thing under my bed. I was really only sitting with this new group because there was safety in numbers. We ate lunch and sat beside each other in the classes we had together, but I never hung out with them after school. They would ask me to sleepovers and trips to the mall, but I always said no. I'd learned a hard lesson from Rai. With friendship came expectations, and I couldn't and wouldn't be able to repay whatever kindness friends would show me. So it just became easier to not have any friends at all.

It was all for the best, I suppose. It was hard for me to do the kind of normal things that most everyone else did, because there was no way I could have anyone over to my house with a hungry monster under my bed. And I was too broke to go to the mall or do anything that cost a lot of money. I could've been upset, but when you're the girl with a monster under her bed you learn how to set priorities pretty quickly. And being popular wasn't anywhere on my list.

Sophomore year I met Andy.

Andy was in my second period math class. He wore glasses and had a gap between his front teeth that I thought was cute. The first day I sat down he turned around and grinned at me, all freckles and gap and glasses. "Hi, I'm Andy."

"Tamara," I said.

"You have really pretty skin," he said before turning around. At first I wondered if it was supposed to be a dig of some sort. I was one of the few black girls at Belleview High. But then after class he smiled at me again, warm and friendly. "See you tomorrow."

At lunch I asked a girl I sat with, Merry, about him. "Oh, Andy is nice. He was in my biology class last year. Why?"

"He said my skin was pretty," I said and stared down at my sandwich. Out loud, it sounded lame, like I couldn't take a compliment.

And from Merry's twisted lips, she thought the same thing. "Tam, he probably likes you. You know, me and Jamie sometimes see him at the mall. Why don't you come with us? Jamie wanted to go shopping for new shoes this weekend. You might see Andy."

I shook my head, the old fear rising up fast and hard. What if I went to the mall and everybody wanted to come back to my house afterward? What if they walked into my room and sat down on my bed, only to have the monster reach out and grab them? It seemed like such a silly fear to have, but I'd pretty much lost my last friend because I couldn't just be normal. There was no way I was going to go through that again.

It was just better to not even try.

And even though I knew that having a boyfriend and liking someone was just as dangerous as having a friend, I started to look forward to math class, which was stupid because I hate math. But there was something about Andy that I really liked. He wasn't cute and he was skinny and awkward looking just like most of the guys at school. But Andy was funny, and nice in such an effortless way. It was good to have those few minutes with him before and after class.

Most importantly, he made me feel normal, which is a hard thing to feel when you live with a monster under your bed.

"Hey, you going to homecoming?" Andy asked me one day, out of the blue.

"Yeah, maybe. Probably not."

"You should go," he said. "Do you want to go with me?"

"Yes." I said it before my brain could tell me to say no.

That night, I went home to tell my mom about having a date to homecoming. She smiled, and then gave me a wad of cash. "You're going to need a dress. I have to work this weekend, but maybe you can go with those friends of yours from school. You should give them a call. You stay home too much."

She was right. So I did.

The weekend before homecoming I went to the mall with Merry and Jamie, where me and Jamie bought dresses and then ate cinnamon rolls as big as our heads while Merry and Jamie talked about how fun and cool Andy was and how much fun we were all going to have. Then we bought shoes and lacy underthings and body lotions that smelled like fruit salad. Merry and Jamie were going to homecoming as a couple, a fact that had scandalized some of the people at school, but they were way more excited than me and the feeling was contagious.

The week before homecoming, I couldn't focus. In math class, Andy would smile at me and say things like "I'm really looking forward to Saturday." I just smiled and said nothing, even though I felt like pure energy, a blue bolt of potential for change. Everything could be different after this dance. I could have a boyfriend. I could have friends.

I could be normal, even with a monster under my bed.

The homecoming game was during the day, and I went with Merry and Jamie. The football team lost terribly, but I barely noticed. I was too excited for the dance.

After, Jamie's mom picked us up we all went to her house to get ready. Merry helped me do my makeup while Jamie did my hair. Jamie asked me to give her cornrows so I did, and she looked silly and amazing at the same time. Merry's hair was too short to do much with, but I did help her tie her tie while Jamie laughed at us. We ordered pizza and ate it carefully so that we wouldn't get sauce on our clothes. We laughed and told jokes, and everything was perfect.

And then we got to the dance.

I walked in, expecting it to be sort of like one of those movies. Soft music. Slow motion as my eyes met Andy's across the room.

But, instead what I saw was Andy grinding on Karrie Kroft, a blonde girl with boobs the size of cantaloupes, while an old Ke$ha song played.

It was nothing like I'd imagined.

"Hey, are you okay?" Merry asked as her eyes followed my line of sight.

"Yeah, I'm cool," I said, but it was a lie. I felt crushed. I thought we'd been going to homecoming as a couple. Maybe I'd misunderstood. Maybe I should go ask him what was going on.

But when his eyes met mine across the dance floor and I raised my hand in a tiny wave, he looked away.

And I felt like the world's biggest loser.

When the song switched Merry gave me a light punch. "I'm going to see what's going on. This isn't cool, Tam."

I watched as she crossed the floor, fists clenched, and walked up to Andy. She pulled him away from Karrie. Their hands flew as they talked, until finally Merry spun on her heel and stormed back to us.

"He's an asshole," she said. Jamie put her arm around Merry, in an attempt to calm her down. "He said that he and Karrie used to go out, and when he saw her here without a date he kind of forgot all about you, Tam." Merry shook her head. "He's such a dick. You're too good for him, you know."

I did know. But that didn't make me feel any better about being in a pretty dress at the homecoming dance all by myself.

I hung out with Merry, who fumed and shot glares in Andy's direction, and Jamie, who tried to cheer me up. But I didn't want to spoil their evening, so about halfway through the night I made a lame excuse about not feeling well and bailed.

I could barely walk in my high heels, so I took them off and began the short trip home. My house wasn't that far from the high school, and it was warm enough out that I almost didn't need a coat. Still, by the time I got home I was heartsore and more than a little angry. I'd looked like a fool, and all for what? A boy?

How silly.

"Hey, Tamara! Hey!"

I stopped and turned around at the sound of my name. Andy came running up behind me.

"Hey, look, I'm sorry. Merry said you'd left. I was going to come over and talk to you, but I just, I lost track of time."

"Whatever," I said, and started walking.

He jogged to catch up and then kept pace. "I just, I shouldn't've blown you off that way."

"It's fine," I said, even though it wasn't. And him smiling and grinning like that, like he hadn't just stomped my heart to pieces so very carelessly, well . . .

It made me even angrier.

I imagined inviting him into my room, him throwing one leg over the windowsill and then the other, followed by the wet gurgle I'd heard the night Rai disappeared.

But no matter how big of a dick Andy was, I still wasn't a murderer.

We walked the rest of the short distance to my house. He talked non-stop, alternately apologizing and justifying the way he blew me off. By the time we arrived, the light on my front porch a welcoming beacon, I was kind of glad that he'd reconciled with his girlfriend.

"Hey, good luck with Karrie," I said, polite even when I was getting dumped for another girl.

"Oh, yeah, about that. We aren't really a thing. Turns out, she was just waiting for her boyfriend."

Suddenly, the way he chased me down as I left made a lot more sense. I was second place.

I didn't like being second place.

"Oh, hey, my mom is home," I said. "But, maybe, you can climb in my window?"

He straightened, and a smile spread across his face. "Yeah?"

"Yeah," I said, trying to make it sound sexy and not angry.

I walked inside, taking my time getting to my room. There was a note from Mom on the fridge "Over at Rob's. Be home late." Rob, Mom's new boyfriend.

Even she wasn't allowed to have sleepovers.

Once inside I got into my pajamas, not even bothering to wash the make-up off of my face. The night was warm and the air conditioner was off.

I opened my window. "Give me a minute to turn off my light," I said into the darkness.

"Okay," came the whispered reply.

I crawled into bed, sitting in the middle of my island of safety, and clicked off the light, my heart pounding.

I was really going to do this.

After a few heartbeats, Andy climbed through my window.

"You know, I actually thought you were mad at me. Most girls wouldn't like being treated like that."

"I'm not like most girls." Except, I was. I'd put on a dress and make up and gotten my hopes up over a stupid boy. A boy who hadn't even noticed, not really.

"No?" he asked with a laugh. His voice had gotten huskier. Andy put one foot, then the other on the floor, and still he was there, joking and laughing. I kept waiting for the wet gurgle, the monster swallowing Andy whole. "What makes you different?"

"I have a monster under my bed."

Andy laughed and sat on the edge of my bed, his feet firmly planted on the floor. "You are so funny."

He leaned in, his eyes glimmering in the low light. I didn't want to kiss him, and I leaned back a little.

Where was my monster?

"What's wrong?" he asked. I sensed more than saw his scowl.

"Nothing. I thought . . ." I thought what? That I had a monster under my bed? That my kitten and best friend from eighth grade had both been eaten?

What if I'd been wrong this whole time?

My anger faded away and I took a deep breath. "You should go," I said.

"Really?"

"Yeah. I was . . . I was wrong, Andy. I'm sorry."

He stood, angrily. "Yeah, fine, whatever."

"Maybe we can hang out later?" I said, hope in my voice. Because even though I didn't want to kiss him, I also didn't want him to be mad at me. I wasn't sure why. He'd been a dick to me. Still, the thought of him leaving angry tore me up a little inside.

"Not likely. Effing tease," he said, climbing to his feet and stomping to the window.

There was a loud thump as Andy hit the floor.

"Hey, what the hell?"

It was the last thing Andy ever said. There was another thump, and then the wet gurgling sound that had haunted my nightmares ever since Rai had gone missing all those years ago.

Only, this time, it didn't sound nearly as bad.

Almost, friendly.

I turned on my light and looked around my room. I'd expected to see blood, maybe some torn clothing.

Nothing.

I turned the light off and lay in the dark. I should've lain awake, I should've wondered what had just happened.

I fell asleep incredibly quickly and slept great.

I woke the next morning to a text from Merry, asking if I wanted to hang out. Things between me and Andy might not have worked out, but at least I had friends I could depend on.

I texted her back and went to grab a shower. I jumped out of bed and for some reason looked back, awareness prickling the hairs on the back of my neck.

Peeking out from under my bed, just enough that I must've missed it last night when I turned on the light, was a man's dress shoe with a foot still inside.

The sound of a burp came from under my bed, the kind of burp people let loose after a large meal. I stared at the foot for a long moment, an emotion part panic and part fear rising up in me.

I took a deep breath and shoved it back down. I got a hanger from my closet and pushed the shoe under the bed, scampering backwards when something within the shadows snatched at it.

I sat there staring at my bed for a long time. Then, I went to take a shower.

I had friends now. Real friends.

I couldn't keep them waiting.

Justina Ireland enjoys dark chocolate, dark humor, and is not too proud to admit that she's still afraid of the dark. She lives with her husband, kid, and dog in Pennsylvania. She is the author of *Vengeance Bound* and *Promise of Shadows*.

Want more? Find a Q&A with Justina on page 246.

Heroin(e)

Kelly Fiore

IF SHE WERE A VERB, IT WOULD BE "BLOOM."

That's how she feels when she enters my bloodstream. Like she's blossoming outward through my veins, petals raining from the sky like some kind of doped-up flower girl in a wedding held just for me and my fix.

I don't usually call her by her given name, but when I do, I always add the "e" at the end.

Heroine.

My savior.

Tonight, she's in my pocket as I'm shuffling along the pavement, my Chucks scraping each crack in the sidewalk like there's nothing I want more than to break my mother's back. It's not really that—I just don't think I can lift my legs any higher. Once I get back to my room,

I'll try to take my time. I'll try to enjoy setting up my rig, cooking the dope, drawing its juices up into the syringe. I'll try not to rush the process, my heart in my throat, my pulse racing like I'm about to discover first love or the New World.

I didn't start with Heroine, of course. She's my forever after, but she wasn't my once upon a time.

No, I started the same way most of us did—at home, at night, with friends. The orange prescription bottle is as familiar to high school parties as the red Solo cup. The oblong white pills were first, then the larger round ones, then the tiny white circles. Vikes, Percs, then Oxys.

First is the worst.

Second is the best.

Third is the one that's better than the rest.

I mean, don't get me wrong. All of them felt like their own version of drinking a hot beverage in the dead of winter—the way that heat filters in through your body, like sunshine from the inside out?

Yeah. All the good shit feels that way.

It's the difference between partly cloudy and a cloudless sky. The more light, the more warmth, the better. I'm always chasing that buttery goodness that feels like it's melting your very being as it drains down through your body.

There isn't a dragon to chase, that's for damn sure—there's nothing that terrifying until you're dope sick.

Then?

Well, then it's all monsters in the night and beasts in the streets. That's when you could claw off your own skin. That's when you could forget your own name.

Well, almost forget anyway.

Greer Maxwell. She was a fine identity for most of my eighteen years of life. Upstanding family. Private school in the Baltimore suburbs. Cheerleader. Honor Society member. Class Secretary.

Greer was a party girl behind the scenes, though. And that's when Max came out. It's what everyone started calling me.

Max.

The blond girl who, somehow, still had a Caribbean tan in the dead of winter. Who could afford Oxys long after they skyrocketed in price. Who had the best parties. Who lied to her parents. Who snuck out at night. Who started caring more about dope than anything else in the world. Who chose to leave home when Mom and Dad handed down the ultimatum.

I've only been on the streets for three months. And, really, let's be honest—these aren't technically "the streets." I'm at an old Econo Lodge-turned-independently-owned-flophouse that's maybe ten miles from my high school. When I squint and look out the window and to the left, I can almost see the Bromo-Seltzer tower.

This is Baltimore—the drugs and their lovers are interspersed with gas stations and Dollar Generals.

I don't really like it here, but I can't go home until I've agreed to go into treatment. My parents gave me pamphlets for a place in upstate New York. Lakeland? Land O' Lakes? Candyland?

It's been a long time since I've eaten.

It's been a long time since I've played games.

I make it to the motel parking lot just as the sun is setting. You already know what this shithole looks like, but for kicks, here's the sitch—two stories, exterior doors, large rectangular windows with a sliding latch and mustard-yellow black-out curtains drawn across every single occupied unit. There are a few windows with cracks webbing across their glass. There aren't bullet holes that I can see, but I've heard enough shots at night to believe that's the reason.

I'm on the second floor, all the way to the left. Room 299. There is no 300.

This is a motel with actual keys, not key cards. This is also a motel with rodents and insects, along with bottom feeders of a completely different variety.

But I don't mind my room's location—I'd rather be above than below.

I let myself in the room, holding my breath against the initial onslaught of the stench. There are a couple things you can't avoid when you're using dope on a regular basis—one of them is the fumes of decay. Decaying food. Decaying body. Decaying life. I suck in through my mouth and exhale through my nose, like I'm changing a litter box. Once I'm inside with the door closed, I take smaller breaths until I can inhale through my nose without cringing.

This place is a disaster—I'll be the first one to admit it. Look, when you live in a slum, you treat it like a slum. I throw my purse on the floor on top of a pile of clothes. I see a couple of labels. YSL. Givenchy. I'm surprised I haven't hocked that shit yet—there are a handful of nice secondhand stores downtown, not to mention ThredUp. I think I honestly forgot I had anything left of value.

The room is what you've already pictured. Two queen beds with weird scratchy comforters that are a cross between southwestern style and just plain tacky. Terra Cotta is a common denominator in the room's décor. I flop down on the closest bed and dig the balloons out of my pocket. They're fat and a thrill courses through my body.

BOOM. BOOM. BOOM.

The knock on my door is less of a knock and more of an attack without punctuation.

BOOMBOOMBOOM

It isn't the cops. This is just how Jazz knocks. He is a physical presence, even when he isn't present.

"Coming."

I don't know Jazz's last name. I know that he's got more ink than most teens I've met—enough that I can only assume he's been getting tattoos since he was way younger than the average person who's covered in tattoos. I find his rebellion as enticing as his dope hook-ups, which is saying a lot. He gets great dope.

KELLY FIORE

When I open the door, he's leaning on the jamb like he belongs there. His shaggy hair is dirty blond—darker than mine, but not by much. The gauges in his ears are about the size of nickels and, despite the meth he's been dabbling in more and more, that smile is still as white and perfect as mine is.

Jazz and I are cut from the same cloth—or similar cloth, anyway. He's from Connecticut, but followed his older brother down here for school. He dropped out once he realized that a diploma wasn't going to pay his bills—bills being the cost of his habit.

We met three months ago and I think I love him.

Well, some days, I love him.

Today I love him.

"Yo."

He smiles at me and I wish that alone could give me the melty feeling I'm after. But my eyes skate down to my hand, still tightly gripping the balloons. I won't tell you how I got them, but I will tell you I'm broke. You can draw your own conclusions.

Jazz's eyes lower to my hand and I know he knows.

"You hooked up?"

I give a half-shrug, then widen the door. Truth is, there's nothing better than having an expert shoot you up and Jazz never misses the vein. He's like an artist.

He follows, shutting the door behind him.

"You were gonna hold out on me?"

He asks it like a question, but he knows. Hell yes, I was gonna hold out on him. Had he not shown up, I

71

would've cooked up a fat load and enjoyed the entire score all by my lonesome.

But I say, "Naw, baby. I knew you were coming by."

Which is a lie in one way—I didn't know—but true in other ways, since he always comes by. There's always something Jazz can get from me, no matter the day. Today, he can get high.

He falls onto the bed with a groan, then rolls over on his right side and scrubs a hand down his face.

"This day's been a bitch, man. I spent the whole morning at the intersection of Pratt and Lombard. My 'Any Kindness Helps' sign wasn't cutting it today."

Jazz is the one who taught me how to panhandle—there are a few rules that are important to follow in order to attract donations while standing at an intersection. According to Jazz, you need to look innocent—like a kid down on their luck or the girl next door.

Next, you need to be clean—showered, if possible, and wearing decent clothes. *If your shit doesn't look buttoned up*, Jazz says, *you look like a bum*. This way, people think you're just waiting for your break and hoping to get a little help along the way. It's the difference between looking like a homeless junkie and looking like someone who just needs a hand back up.

I open the desk drawer and pull my kit out from its home next to the obligatory Bible—even junkie hotel rooms can't duck out on that requirement. In a small rectangular Tupperware container are the icons of my religion—a handful of syringes, cotton, two lighters, and a stainless steel spoon. The handle is bent over and has a delicate floral pattern.

It's one of my parents' spoons.

I can remember the day Mom and Dad sat me down and asked me if I was using. Mom already knew. Still, she sat in the family room next to Dad on the couch and gave me the same concerned look he gave me—the only difference, really, was in the eyes. Mom's held a resignation that Dad had yet to succumb to.

"We want you to go to Lakeland," Dad had said, his voice firm but tinged with hope. "It's a treatment facility. They can help get you well."

"And if I don't go?" I'd sneered.

I was jonesing for a fix that day and had skipped school for the umpteenth time. I'd kept checking my phone for a text from my hookup, so I only remember half of the conversation.

"Then you need to find another place to live," Mom had said quietly. Dad turned to stare at her and I read the surprise in his expression. Mom, on the other hand, was resolute. Her arms were crossed over her chest to shield her heart—to keep it from feeling anything for me that would cause her to falter.

I almost respected it—at least until that night when I was wandering the harbor and cursing that I'd chosen to take off on a winter night instead of a summer evening.

But that was the night I met Jazz—the night he took me back to his buddy's loft in Hampden, which ended up actually just being a place they were squatting in temporarily. The night he stroked my hair and pressed his lips against both my closed eyes just before he shot me up. That night, it felt like he was soothing me—like he was *parenting* me. It was exactly what I needed at that exact moment. I was disproportionately grateful.

And I'm still grateful. Grateful enough to share what I scored today. It doesn't get more grateful than that.

He rolls off the bed now, pulling half of the comforter down off the end. It ripples to the floor, folding in on itself. It looks like the bed is shedding its skin.

Jazz walks over to me and takes the kit from my hands, pressing a brief kiss to my forehead. Tonight, it feels less like warmth and more like he's thanking me. Like he owes me or something.

"How much you get?"

I blink at him, then hold out the bloated little balloons. Their brilliant red has dulled in the palm of my sweaty hand. I've been gripping them so tight that, if they'd been living and breathing, they'd have been dead long before now. Jazz examines their size and shape before nodding his approval.

"This'll do us good, baby. Who'd you score from?"

I give a half-shrug. "Nate."

Jazz wrinkles his nose. Nate isn't one of his favorite people. He'd dislike him even more if he knew what I did to get it.

"You sure it ain't cut with something?"

I cross my arms. "I dunno. Nate said it was good shit. I just thought . . ."

I trail off and Jazz ducks a bit to meet my gaze. I hate when he questions me like this, like I'm too stupid to score on my own.

"You still did good, baby," he says. "I just hate the idea of you copping without me there."

He steps a little closer and cups my chin.

"I want to be able to protect you."

I nod and he lets go of my face, his attention already drawn back to the kit, the balloons, and the promise of a night-long vacation. I don't blame him. I'm distracted by it, too.

I watch Jazz dump the contents of one balloon into the bowl of the spoon, adding a little water before sparking the lighter beneath. What people don't understand about this life is that it's not just about the high—it's about the build up. The anticipation. The time it takes to cook your dope, to load up your rig, to slam it home—well, all of it is like foreplay.

Jazz pulls the murky brown liquid up into a syringe and reaches for my arm. I give it willingly. When it comes to Jazz— when it comes to dope—I seem to give up everything willingly. He examines the crook of my elbow with the precision of a doctor, with the eyes of an artist. He's trying to find the best way for me to get the best high.

He presses hard on a vein deep beneath the surface, alternating pressure until the skin around it begins to turn red. When he reaches for his belt, I know we're ready and I can feel my heart speed its pace in preparation.

Jazz's belt is black leather with metal studs, but the interior is a softer suede. That's the part I feel when he loops it around my upper arm. He pulls it tight, then hands me the tail to hold onto. Most people squeeze someone's hand when they get a shot. I squeeze the end of my makeshift tourniquet. Sometimes, when it's hard to get a good vein and he has to poke around, I'll bite down on it in an attempt to hold in my screams.

But today isn't one of those days. The vein pops up beautifully. It reminds me of spring, of plants breaking ground and reaching for the sun. I watch Jazz press the needle to my skin, watch the flush of red blood swim up into the syringe – a sign that he's hit the vein on the first try. I loosen the belt from my arm just as he pushes the stopper in one steady move. The contents—my blood and my drugs—empty into my body.

The bloom isn't instantaneous. But it's close.

The heat begins in my elbow and makes its journey down to my fingers and up into my shoulder. Its descent through my body is swift and miraculous. Every time, it feels like rebirth. Every time, it feels like home.

I watch through my haze as Jazz cooks his own dose. He pulls up his sleeve. The scabs along his knuckles and between his fingers show failed attempts at shooting up, but it's the bruised and bloody patches on his arm that look the worst. Some of them are practically pits in his body, like bullet-less bullet holes. He's like a veteran of some kind of war, wearing wounds of his own making.

It takes Jazz longer to find his vein than mine, which isn't really surprising. I've only been using daily for six months and my veins are still viable for the most part. Jazz has been using for years—I have no idea how many—and his are shot.

Soon, I'm nodding off a bit. I'm not sure where exactly he ends up finding a vein—I know he's used his neck before and between his toes. But it doesn't really matter. I'm feeling the kind of euphoria that makes you paralyzed with it—you're both weightless and heavy, both dark and light. You're all kinds of contradictions and, while you want to stay awake to experience it, you can't help but doze off.

After an amount of time that I couldn't possibly estimate, Jazz puts his hand on my shoulder and helps me lay back in bed.

"You're about to fall forward, baby. I don't want you to get hurt."

I settle into the flat pillow and manage to ignore the reeking scent of unwashed hair. Jazz climbs into bed next to me. I feel his weight on my right side as the bed sinks, then his body heat as he presses against me. I start to drift off again as his hand runs up my thigh.

This time, I fall asleep—at least, asleep enough to dream. This doesn't happen all that often, but when it does, the vision always feels uncomfortably real.

In my dream, the only face I can see is my grandmother's. Nana's been dead for years, but I still remember going to the hospital and saying goodbye to her. She was shackled to the bed by the tubes and wires hooked up to her body. There was an IV dispensing clear fluid down into the drip chamber and each *drop drop drop* felt like another second that took us closer to her death.

Her skin was papery when I touched her hand. Mom leaned in and kissed Nana's cheek, tears streaming down her face. Dad stood in the corner of the room, stoic and somber, which is pretty much his M.O. when it comes to tragedy. If Nana could have spoken, she would have told him to relax. She would have told him he could use a drink.

Over the years, I've thought a lot about what she would have said to me, too, but I always come up with nothing.

But in my dream, she speaks.

At first, I am focusing my gaze on the needle in her arm—the crusted blood along the gauze strip, the white tape bordered by fuzzy lint from her blanket or sweater.

"This is the only way for me now. But you and I are different."

The sound of Nana's voice is less scratchy and faint than in years prior. It's more like the strong, lilting brogue I remember like my own name.

"When you're ready to say goodbye, then you let it take you. You let it save anything but your life."

I glance up at the dripping IV bag.

It's morphine. My heroine's partner-in-crime.

I look back at Nana and this time she's smiling.

"You can't get warm, so the drugs can do it. You can't get happy, so the drugs can do it. You can't get hungry, so the drugs can do it. But the role they play is for an audience of the dying."

There is a pause. She stares at me. I stare at her.

"And there aren't any heroes left to save you. You can only save yourself."

When I wake up, my body aches in a way that makes me dread opening my eyes at all. When I do, I realize it's light outside. We'd pulled the curtains shut last night, but I can see a sliver of the day between them. I glance over at the clock—just after 8 am. I'd slept through the night. Any trace of my high, any trace of that hazy warmth is gone.

What's left is only cold and bad and dark and angry. What's left feels like a cave I can't crawl my way out of.

It doesn't take long for the dope sweat to set in. Now, I'm usually sick whenever I get up in the morning, at least until I get my first dose. It's a special brand of perspiration—more greasy and slimy than normal sweat. Nothing like the kind you get from physical activity or healthy pursuits. No, it's the kind that makes you want to slide out of your own skin.

Jazz's leg is thrown over mine and it feels suffocatingly heavy. I manage to wriggle out from underneath him. He snorts out a snore, then settles into the pillows.

The sweat doesn't drip from my body, but seems to recirculate through my pores. There's only one thing that will make it go away. There's only one thing that will prevent it from getting worse.

I scoot from the edge of the bed to the floor and kneel next to the nightstand, its shiny pressboard gleaming almost unnaturally from the morning shaft of light slicing through the room. The balloons aren't there. The spoon, the whole kit is gone. I can feel my heart begin to race and I travel, on my knees, toward the dresser.

There, I find the spoon, the lighter, my syringes.

And three emptied red balloons, barely shells of their former selves.

Jazz.

He used all of it last night.

I could cry if I had the energy to do anything but vomit. That was supposed to get me through the day. I've been trying to pace myself. Yesterday, I ran out of cash. Yesterday, I paid for my fix with something else.

From my position on the floor, I glance up and catch my image in the smeared mirror above the dresser. I blink and look again. It's been a long time since I've seen anything but a flash of my reflection. They only mirrors I usually see now are covered in white powder or broken on abandoned cars.

My tan is gone. My eyes are the same clear blue, but no one would call my hair blonde – not at first glance, anyway. My lips are chapped in a way that makes them look shattered.

I move my gaze and see Jazz still sprawled and snoring in the bed behind me. He's naked from the waist up and his tattoos look anything but sexy today. The blood on his arms makes him look like he's seen some kind of battle. We may have come from the same worlds before, but he feels like a complete stranger in the sober light of day.

I look down and around me at the clothes on the floor, the rotting food, the disastrous evidence of my spectacular downfall. I am a statistic. I would laugh or roll my eyes if I felt any kind of emotion other than despair.

Slowly, so that I don't fall over, I pull on old pajama pants with hot pink X's and O's and a dirty Towson University sweatshirt. I find a pair of flip-flops under a pile of pizza boxes. As I shove my phone and cigarettes in my pocket, I don't look back at myself in the mirror. Instead, I crack the door and slip outside into the sunshine, squinting against its onslaught.

Baltimore mornings are still cold when you're up this early—up with the worker bees of the city. The scurry below on the sidewalk and the line at the bus station is an undeniable reminder that so many people live a completely different kind of existence than mine. They have places to go, jobs to work at, an expectation to fulfill.

HEROIN(E)

I, on the other hand, have a boy in my bed and a distinct lack of dope in my veins.

I move to the metal barrier that edges the concrete area outside the motel room doors. If this were a different kind of hotel, I might call this area a balcony. But this is not that kind of hotel. Now, I grasp the cold metal with both hands and lean back. The stretch in my limbs is soothing for the briefest of moments and then, just like that, it is gone. In its place is a half-assed attempt at standing and breathing and living, all of which feel excruciatingly hard.

There was a time when this existence felt like freedom. Now, it feels like prison—and the metal bars I'm clinging to are doing that metaphor plenty of favors. I pull my pack of Camel Filters from my pocket and light one up, taking a long drag. I think of my grandmother again—how the lung cancer had spread through her body like heat lightning: sporadic, but beyond efficient. She'd always said smoking was her biggest regret. She always told me not to do it.

I wish smoking was my biggest regret. I wish I could say that smoking was the worst thing, the most destructive thing I'd ever done.

Inside my front sweatshirt pocket, my phone buzzes. I dig it out, peering at it. A number flashes across the screen and I feel a little sick.

It's Nate.

I could ignore it— not answer and sit down on the

82

steps and cry, trying not to think about how sick I'm going to be in an hour or in two or in five.

But I answer it instead.

"Hey, Nate," I say, my voice almost raspy.

"Yo, bae—how you doin' this morning? I swallow back a little bit of vomit and the dry echo of the pack of Camels I smoked last night.

"Not a whole lot. Why you up this early?"

I hear him suck in a drag through the receiver. It could be a cigarette. It could be something far better.

"I was thinking I could stop by—maybe we could have a little chat like we did yesterday."

I bite down on my bottom lip. "Jazz is here."

Nate exhales. "Yeah, I know. He texted me a few minutes ago. Suggested I stop by with another few balloons. Said you'd make it worth my while."

I blink rapidly. Jazz hates Nate. He hates when I spend time with him. Now he's offering me up as, what? Some kind of screwed up sacrifice?

"I . . ." I trail off, unsure of what to say. Behind me, the motel room door cracks open. I see Jazz, shirtless, squinting out into the light.

"Whatcha doing, baby?" he asks. His voice is scratchy like mine. I pull the phone away from my ear.

"Nate said he just talked to you? About coming over here?"

Jazz shrugs. "Yeah—figured it'll give us a chance to get some good shit."

He ambles outside, his feet bare like his chest, and moves closer to me.

"I was thinking that we could have a little fun — the three of us . . ."

He trails off a bit, but one of his eyebrows is lifted suggestively. I almost stutter, feeling indignant. Then Jazz leans even closer.

"I know what you did yesterday to get those balloons, Max. And that was some of the best dope I've had in a long time."

He scrubs a hand over his pale face, his bleary eyes, his pinched and puckered mouth. I put the phone back to my ear.

"I'll text you," I tell Nate, not waiting for him to respond before I press END.

"What do you think, baby?" Jazz asks. He wraps his arms around my waist and rests his chin on my shoulder. His grip is loose, but it feels like a vise. It feels like I'm trapped here, without a way to say no.

And I want to say no. More than anything. I want to say no to Nate and Jazz and the balloons in my future.

I want to say no to my heroine. I really, actually do.

"Can I think about it?" I ask Jazz. His focus is sort of scattered, meaning that it's not directed at me. He is starting to sweat, too. I know exactly how he's feeling.

"Sure," he says, dropping his arms from my waist. I can tell he isn't pleased — his tone completely changes.

"I'm going to get in the shower," he says, turning his back and heading into the room. I fight the urge to reach out and pull him against me. I want to feel something solid so very badly, but even I know that it can't be Jazz. It probably never was.

"I'll be in in a minute," I say, but he's already closing the door on my words. I turn around and look out at the street. The asphalt seems to practically glow — its own version of a Yellow Brick Road.

There's no place like home.

There's no place like home.

Home.

I let myself savor the word for a second. I think about the things I haven't let myself think about for weeks. For longer than that.

My bed with its fluffy down comforter.

My walls with their pale peach paint that perfectly matched my armchair's upholstery.

My cat snuggling on my feet as though they were pillows made just for her.

My parents' faces the night I left.

I want to go home. I don't want to do this anymore.

My hands are trembling as I scroll through my phone. I'm close to puking up whatever food is left in my system, which can't be much. I don't even know what I'll say to them. I'm wordless, but I'm still searching for the number in my short list of contacts.

One finger hovers over the word HOME. I bite my lip and close my eyes as I let that finger fall. And then I exhale.

Ring.

Maybe they aren't there.

Ring.

Maybe I'll get the machine. Should I leave a message?

Ring.

Maybe I could just—

"Hello?"

Never before or since has anything sounded better than my mother's voice on the phone at that moment. That word—that "hello" was tentative and almost whispered, like it was said in disbelief.

Like she'd read the caller ID before she picked up.

"Mom?"

My voice is barely a croak. On the other end of the line, I hear her suck in a sharp breath.

"Greer?"

For a long moment, I hold on to that word. My name. Then I swallow and start nodding.

"It's me."

"Oh, god—honey, how are you? Are you okay? Where are you?"

I keep nodding uselessly and the tears start coursing down my face. They feel like a shower. They feel like I'm being washed clean.

"I want to come home," I manage to choke out. I touch a hand to my cracked chapped lips. I want to feel these words as they come out of my mouth. Then I will believe them.

"I need help."

I can hear my mother begin to cry, hear her call for my father as I sit down on the curb. It feels cold through my pajamas. Around me, the world is waking up to its morning routine. Cars drive by. The traffic light on the corner cycles through its colors. People are starting to walk past me on their way to somewhere else.

I want to be on my way somewhere else, too.

And for the first time in a long time, I think I might be.

Kelly Fiore has a BA in English from Salisbury University and an MFA in Poetry from West Virginia University. She received an Individual Artist Award from the Maryland State Arts Council in 2005 and 2009. Kelly's poetry has appeared in Small Spiral Notebook, Samzidada, Mid Atlantic Review, Connotation Press, and the Grolier Annual Review. Her books include *Taste Test* and *Just Like the Movies* both from Bloomsbury USA and the forthcoming *Thicker Than Water* from HarperTeen in 2016.

Want more? Find a Q&A with Kelly on page 248.

Canary

Demitria Lunetta

H<small>E WAS THE MOST BEAUTIFUL BOY</small> Lizzy had ever seen.

She watched him as he lay in the sun, his yellow hair catching the sunlight and shimmering, as if it were made of gold. His skin was a shade she'd never seen before—light brown, like the cakes her mama fried up for breakfast. He looked to be about her age, fifteen or sixteen, maybe older.

She'd walked down to the swimming hole to take a bath and discovered the golden boy and two more people she'd never seen before. The others played in the water, screeching and making enough noise to wake the dead. There was a girl, another shade she'd never seen, darker than the brown of the trees, with deep black hair cut short like a boy's. She looked so strange, and yet

Lizzy's attention was always brought back to the boy in the sun. The golden boy. She barely took in that there was another boy, giving him no more than a cursory glance. He was nothing extraordinary, pale and bony, with light brown hair like hers.

Her entire life, she couldn't remember meeting anyone who wasn't a cousin or an aunt or an uncle, kin to her in some way. She was so shocked, she stood in the trees and just watched them in silence.

She had no idea how long she stood there. Eventually, the boy's kin came out of the water and sat in the sun to dry. They wore clothing while they bathed, and Lizzy thought that was just silly. The boy himself wore short pants and no shirt, and Lizzy found herself blushing as she stared at his well-muscled arms and chest. She'd seen her brothers naked as the day they were born but for some reason, this boy's near-nakedness made her feel hot, like that time she had a fever and Mama gave her those nasty herbs to drink.

When they talked, their voices were clear and high, but she had trouble understanding them at first. It was like they hadn't quite learned how to speak properly. After listening for a while she started to make out words and then whole sentences. "Isn't this just the best?" the girl asked, sitting on a strange, brightly colored blanket. She stretched her long legs and arms before collapsing back, her hands tucked behind her head. She wore bright red undergarments, a separate top and bottom. Lizzy had never seen a red so bright, or underclothes so small.

The other boy said something that Lizzy didn't understand, it sounded like, "Tress-pass-in" and he seemed a little scared. But the girl laughed and hugged him and told him not to worry. She said, "This is so off the beaten path, even the park rangers don't come around here. Look, we'll hang here until Evan recovers, then follow the stream down to the falls. It's beautiful down there."

Lizzy didn't know what park or rangers were, but then her boy said, "Thanks, Kendall," and raised his eyebrows. "We're not all super jocks."

"Look, I found this place last time I came hiking in the park and I couldn't stay long. I wanted to share it with Chris and I didn't know you were visiting this weekend . . ." she trailed off.

"Are we even still in the park?" the boy, Chris, asked.

The girl shrugged and laid back down. They'd brought more than one of those small, brightly colored blankets, one for each of them. Lizzy thought they meant to take naps, but after a while, the girl and the other boy stood, joined hands and went off into the woods, giggling. Lizzy thought for a moment on what to do. She'd been gone a long time and her brothers were bound to come looking for her eventually. She looked at the sky, the sun at high noon. The wedding was soon and if she went missing her pa would skin her alive.

She sighed. She could just turn around and head home and leave the beautiful boy to himself. Maybe no one would find him.

She couldn't be sure though, not with the wedding today. All of her kin would be coming in from all over the mountain and there's no way she could be certain that the boy would be safe. She took a deep breath and stepped into the clearing.

He didn't notice her at first and she tentatively called out a "hello."

The boy's head pivoted toward her and he did a double take, jumping up off his blanket and backing away. "Holy shit . . . where did you come from, I nearly pissed my pants." He let out a little laugh and rubbed his hand through his golden hair, taking a good look at her. He took another step back, his shocked look returning. "What happened to your face?"

It took a moment for Lizzy to understand what he'd asked, his way of talking was so strange. The question itself didn't bother her. She knew she wasn't much to look at, her brothers told her that often enough. When her mama was giving birth, Lizzy decided she wasn't ready to be born so Aunt Agatha, the midwife, had to reach in with a special tool and grab her out. It left Lizzy's face an odd shape, like a potato, her sister always said.

That's why her sister was getting married today instead of her. When Aunt Mildred died in childbirth, Uncle Jasper needed a new wife to look after the young ones, and Papa said he could have his choice of his girls. He took one look at Lizzy and offered for Grace right on the spot. Never mind she was a year younger and had a head full of chicken feathers. Never mind she wasn't as strong or as practical as Lizzy. At least she had a pretty face.

The boy started talking again, "Oh look, I didn't mean it. You just scared me. I didn't know anyone else was out here besides us."

Lizzy nodded slowly. He was taller than she thought he'd be, and up close his skin looked so smooth. Even Grace's skin wasn't that perfect, not after she had a bad bout of the pox and picked at the scabs.

Lizzy looked into the boy's eyes and gasped. Up close, they were extraordinary . . . so dark. Everyone she knew had watery blue eyes that always lightened with age. The oldest of her kin were all blind, their gaze a milky white. This boy though, his eyes were like deep tunnels. Endless.

She looked down at her feet. "I'm Lizzy," she said quietly, shy.

"I'm Evan," he said, and she looked up in time to catch a brilliant smile.

"Evan." She tried the strange name out. It felt good to say. "I ain't never heard of a boy called Evan 'fore."

"Really?" His face scrunched in confusion, then relaxed into an easy grin. "Oh, are you making fun of me? Because it's a girl's name too? I know, I get that a lot." He shrugged. "I guess I deserve that after I acted like such an ass. What are you doing out here anyway? Hiking?" He looked Lizzy up and down. "Are you doing some kind of reenactment thing . . . like those civil war people? Your costume is pretty great."

Lizzy didn't know what to say, so she nodded and said, "Thank ya." Her mama told her sister Grace that whenever she didn't know what was going on, which was fairly often, to nod, smile, and always be polite. It always worked out for her. It worked out for Lizzy now because the golden boy, Evan, gave her another smile. It made her feel a gentle glow and gave her courage.

"How'd ya and your kin get up here?" she asked, curious. She knew there were other people besides her family, people that lived in faraway places. Sometimes her brothers or uncles spotted strangers while hunting farther down the mountain. They always got rid of them before they could make their way up here. She never thought she'd actually get to meet one of them.

"Kin?"

"The other boy and the girl," she told him.

"Oh no, those are just my friends. Chris graduated last year and is spending the summer on campus so I came to visit him, even though I'm still a lowly high-schooler. His new girlfriend Kendall seems nice. She said she knew this amazing place that no one ever goes and it was a really far drive but . . ." He stops and stares at Lizzy, causing her face to warm at his attention. "Sorry. Chris always says I talk too much. Kind of glad you wandered over. I was feeling like the third wheel. I think Kendall thought she'd have Chris all to herself." He shrugs. "Oh well, whatever. Hey, what are you doing here, so far from civilization . . . wait, let me guess . . . there's a historical village or something around here that shows how the coal miners worked back in the day. Kendall took us on that ass-backwards hike; I bet there's a road nearby we could have just taken the car and driven right up."

Lizzy nodded again. She didn't know about roads or what car meant, but she knew all about the mines. "A long time ago my kin used to work the mines . . . but they're all abandoned now," she told Evan. "Ya gotta be careful or ya might fall down a mine shaft."

He looked suddenly worried. "But not right 'round here," she assured him.

"Oh. Good. Hey, maybe I'll check out your village. Do you have a pamphlet or something?"

"Pam-flet?" Lizzy asked.

"Oh sorry. If you're on your break you probably don't want to talk about history and stuff, or carry around pamphlets. Really, the only thing I know about mines is they used to keep a canary in a cage so in case of a natural gas leak they'd get a warning and could clear out. Isn't that awful?"

Lizzy nodded, then shook her head, confused. "Why is that awful?" she asked tentatively.

"Killing an animal like that."

This made no sense to Lizzy, who helped slaughter pigs and often killed and plucked chickens for dinner. "But we're people and animals are animals. They're for eating."

Evan looked genuinely angry. "We don't need to eat animal protein for sustenance. I'm a vegetarian."

"So ya don't eat any animals at all?" Lizzy asked doubtfully.

"No," he said firmly. "To me, animals and people are the same and deserve the same treatment."

Lizzy had never thought of animals as people before, even though she knew the pigs had their own personalities and her uncle Jonathan loved his old hunting hound more than he did his own wife. When the old bitch had her last litter of puppies, he treated them like they were the most precious thing on the mountain, taking care with who got which one. Lizzy's brother Ephraim, who was always a favorite with the uncles, got first pick.

"So what do ya eat?" Lizzy asked, still trying to understand this strange boy.

"Oh, lots of things are vegetarian, really." He walked to small white box, tugged open the top and pulled out a bright blue package.

"Oreos," he said with a grin.

"Or-eee-oes?" Lizzy parroted, uncertain.

"Sure, even though I'm a vegetarian, I've gotta have some junk food." He opened the package, the wrapping crinkling under his touch, and removed three black-brown discs, a stripe of white through the center. Before Lizzy knew what was happening he was standing beside her, placing a few in her hand. His touch made her catch her breath. When he stepped away, he was already chewing and Lizzy quickly placed one of the discs in her mouth.

She couldn't help the noise that escaped her mouth. It was the best thing she had ever tasted. Better than her aunt Ruth's apple cakes. Better than bacon. "I can see why ya'd eat this and not chicken," she said, her mouth full.

Evan laughed. "I know, good, right? They're my favorite."

"Mine too," Lizzy said happily. She wanted to shove the rest in her mouth but she put the remaining two Or-eee-oes in her pocket for later. They were special.

"When do you have to work?" Evan asked.

Lizzy never wanted to leave. She wanted to sit on one of those bright blankets and talk with Evan all day, all week if she could. She wanted to stay there and stare at his perfect teeth and dark eyes.

"I can stay a while longer," she told him with a smile. A whistle came from the woods and her smile dropped.

"Ya gotta go. Now," she told him. "Ya gotta hide."

She started gathering up the strange blankets.

"Hey, wait, what?"

"My brothers. They'll be here real soon." That whistle was Ephraim calling out to his dog, Blackie, and where Ephraim went, Jacob followed.

"Brothers?" Evan asked. His face scrunched in confusion. "You're not from some reenactment group are you?"

Lizzy pushed the blankets into his arms and grabbed the white box so tightly it nearly crumbled in her hands. She didn't have time to marvel at the strange, spongy material. She quickly hid it in the trees and came back to Evan, who still hadn't moved.

"My brothers don't like strangers. If they catch ya here, they'll kill ya."

Evan's lips twitched like he wanted it to be a joke but Lizzy's desperate tone finally got him moving. She pulled him to the trees. "Crouch down real low and don't make a sound. Not a peep," she told him. All hint of a smile was gone from his face, instead it was lined with fear. "If they catch ya, they'll kill ya," she repeated because she didn't think he understood. Not really. This boy who wasn't from the mountain. How could he really understand their ways?

"Lizzy, watcha doin?" Ephraim asked, stepping into the clearing, his shotgun at his side. He never went anywhere without it, would bathe with it . . . if he ever bathed. Lizzy turned slowly around, trying not to look guilty. Blackie broke out of the forest and made a bee-line for Evan's hiding spot, but Lizzy intercepted him, wrapping him in a bear hug.

"I was just gonna take a bath," she said, rubbing Blackie down. "Maybe ya should take one too. I can smell ya from here."

Jacob appeared beside Ephraim. "We ain't got time for a bath. Pa sent us to fetch ya."

"All right then. Call your dog. He's slobbering on me," Lizzy told him and Ephraim whistled for Blackie to heel. Blackie looked over Lizzy's shoulder once with a whine, but obediently went to Ephraim's side.

"What's that?" Jacob asked, pointing to something on the ground. Lizzy's heart stopped. There was a bag she hadn't seen, it wasn't bright like those blankets.

"Don't know," she said cautiously.

Ephraim walked over to it and studied it, considering. He glanced at Jacob. "I think we've got strangers on the mountain."

"Never caught any so far up," Jacob remarked slowly. "Ain't caught any since last year."

"Well they're here now. We gotta hunt them down." Their pa and uncles hated strangers. This was their mountain and had been for a hundred years. They weren't going to let anyone come in and take it away from them.

"But the wedding," Lizzy broke in. "Pa will be real mad if we miss Grace's wedding," she reminded them.

"He'll understand. This is more important . . ." Blackie began to bark and Lizzy's heart dropped, but he wasn't snarling at Evan's hiding spot, he was barking at the far clearing where two figures appeared.

"Oh." The girl, who Evan had called Kendall, let out a gasp of surprise, her mouth in turning into a round O. Chris didn't have time to say anything at all. Without hesitation Jacob and Ephraim raised their guns and fired. Chris was hit in the head and fell to the ground, his face a ruin of skull and blood. Kendall let out a scream; she was only clipped in the shoulder. That would have been Jacob. He wasn't nearly as good a shot as Ephraim.

Lizzy heard a gasp from Evan's hiding place, and then a few quick breaths. Her brothers hadn't noticed though, too intent on the task at hand. All eyes were on Kendall, who sunk to her knees, clutching her shoulder, her look of surprise turning to one of pure pain.

"Better finish her," Ephraim told Jacob, calmly, spitting on the ground.

Jacob took a step closer, while Kendall whimpered. "No. Please. Don't," she pleaded.

"Jacob, ya ain't gotta kill her," Lizzy pleaded. "Maybe we could take her home to Pa. He might say we can keep her. One of the uncles might want her."

"Don't be stupid," Ephraim said. "She ain't family. She don't belong here."

Jacob took a step forward, aimed his gun at her head and pulled the trigger. The shot rang through the forest. He made his way over to her body, shaking his head. "That's a real shame," he said. "She was awful pretty."

They dragged the bodies to the stream and let the current take them down the mountain. They tossed the bag in after them. "C'mon, Lizzy," Ephraim said, grabbing her arm roughly. "We gotta go."

"Yeah," she said. "I just . . . let me catch my breath."

"Ya ain't as soft as all that?" Jacob asked with a wicked grin.

"Leave her," Ephraim said. "Better hurry and collect yourself though Lizzy, or Pa will tan your hide."

"I'll be along shortly," Lizzy told them. She waited a few minutes before walking to Evan's hiding place. She found him huddled, hugging his knees, tears in his eyes. All Lizzy felt was relief. She couldn't help the other two, but she could make sure Evan was safe.

"Ya did real good, not making a noise," she told him, daring to reach out her hand and stroke his hair. Her fingers trembled slightly.

"I hid. I didn't even try to help them. I didn't even look." His dark eyes focused on her. "Chris and Kendall. They're dead, aren't they?" he asked.

Lizzy nodded. "I'm real sorry about that. I . . . once my brothers saw them, there was no other way."

"Why . . . why would they kill them?" he asked, his eyes desperately searching her face.

"Y'all are strangers," she answered. When she saw he still didn't understand, she continued, "After the mines closed down, my kin stayed on the mountain. They tried to move us off but we fought back. Now hardly nobody comes up here."

"But . . . that must have been over a hundred years ago." He rubbed his hands across his face. "No one even knows you're up here anymore. This is protected land."

Lizzy shrugged. "And if they found us, they'd make us leave. That's what pa and all the uncles say. That's why any strangers get killed."

Evan's face crumpled. "Am I . . . are they going to find me?"

"I won't let that happen," she promised. "I gotta go to a wedding."

"A wedding?" he asked. "I don't understand."

"I'll be back though. Don't leave this spot. My kin is all over this mountain. If they see ya, you're dead."

He nodded then.

"After the wedding I'll come back and walk ya out. I'll get ya to a safe place."

He grabbed her hand and squeezed it. "Thank you," he said quietly. Lizzy wished that he'd never have to let go, but she knew the longer she stayed the more likely it was she would get him caught. Soon she stood and quickly walked to the path that would take her home.

It was dark by the time Lizzy made her way back to him. He was still there, still in the same position, rocking back and forth. The night was cool and he hadn't even bothered to wrap one of those blankets around himself.

"Ya got a shirt?" she asked.

"In my bag . . . I don't know where it is." He looked around blankly.

"It's halfway down the mountain by now. Ya gotta cover up though, it's cold."

"I'll use a towel." He tried to drape the blanket over his shoulders but it just fell to the ground. Lizzy did it for him, tying the end in a little knot around his neck, and made him stand. When she started to walk, he followed her without question.

She talked to him, tried to make him talk back. "The wedding was fine. Grace was happy . . . she likes lil' ones and now she's got three to take care of. Oh, and Pa butchered one of the pigs and Mama cooked it up for the wedding dinner but I didn't eat a bite of it. I was thinkin' about being a veg-tar-an like ya. I liked what ya said about animals being the same as people. I think you're right about that." She babbled on, no longer shy. "All my uncles got drunk as skunks, and most of the aunts too. Even the lil' ones were sneaking sips of moonshine."

For a long time, his sniffling was his only reply to her words.

"Why are we going up the mountain?" he asked finally. "The car was way back down there," he motioned vaguely downhill.

"This is the only safe way," she assured him.

"What . . . what about their bodies?" he asked.

"They were put in the stream . . . they'll end up at the falls. Whatever goes over the falls don't come back up."

She paused on the path. "Go on ahead," she told Evan. "Don't be afraid."

He walked in front of her and disappeared into the night. Lizzy heard a creaking noise, followed by a heavy thud and a slow moan. She skirted the opening to the mine shaft and peered down into the hole. In the pale moonlight, she could just make out Evan's face.

"Lizzy," he called up, his voice desperate. "I hurt my ankle. I don't think I can climb out.

"It's okay, Evan. You're safe now. My kin won't find ya. I'm the only one who comes here."

"What...? I need a doctor. I need to call the police." He let out a small, frightened sob. "I'll die down here."

"I'll bring ya food and water. I'll bring ya blankets. I'll be back real soon."

"No, wait." His voice echoed from the mine shaft into the night. "You can't leave me here."

Lizzy whistled as she walked away, filled with more happiness than she'd ever known in her life. Evan had changed everything. He made her see that animals were the same as people. And that meant people were the same as animals.

Just like her uncle with his favorite dog. Just like that canary in the mine.

He now belonged to her.

Demitria Lunetta is the author of the YA sci-fi duology, *In the After* and *In the End*. She holds a BA in Human Ecology and has spent countless hours studying the many ways in which people are capable of bringing about their own destruction. In case the end is near, she always carries a good book and a chocolate bar—the two items essential for post-apocalyptic survival. *In the After* is an American Booksellers Association 2013 ABC Best Books for Children and an Amazon 2013 Top Twenty Teen Book.

Want more? Find a Q&A with Demitria on page 250.

Phantom Heart

Mindy McGinnis

MEDICINE CAN'T EXPLAIN WHY a phantom limb itches in the night, fingers scratching for skin that isn't there. They don't know how to silence the burn in a foot that doesn't exist, the tingle in a hand rotting elsewhere. There is no answer for how a muscle not attached to the body can cramp, causing familiar pain in a limb long estranged from its owner.

They've tried. Severed nerve endings have been cauterized, stumps shortened, entire areas of the brain deadened to stop signals from nowhere. It doesn't work. Instead of relief the afflicted receive fresh pain to compound the suffering, scar tissue piled over trauma.

As far as I know, I'm the first with a phantom heart.

I wasn't aware of my sister until she fell in love with the wrong person. She would've been my twin, our umbilical cords wrapped around each other on our birthday, the same way our limbs intertwined in mother's womb—until I absorbed her. My body was the stronger, but her heart stayed true, living quietly inside of me throughout our childhood. Our lives stayed in step until the moment when my love wandered down the hallway to the band room, hers drawn to the back alley where the roughs snuck a smoke in between classes. There was the smallest tug in my chest as she asserted herself, my body going one direction, her heart another.

When the pathways diverged my life crumbled, odd compulsions sending me into crying jags at the sight of a tattooed arm, hauntingly familiar yet hard to place. My lips would curl around a joint I'd never tasted, arms hungry for a muscled body my own could never desire. A name I didn't want to know echoed through my head and drove me mad, my own love's face fading from sight as I was eaten from the inside for need of someone else. Someone I despised.

Madness loomed. I spent long hours on my bed, hands crossed protectively across my chest, willing common sense to prevail over emotion. Honesty drove me to my parents, an outpouring of feelings not my own and the conviction that another resided inside me earned nothing more than earlier curfews and appointments with specialists. But the doctors they took me to treated the mind and not the heart, and so they did me no good.

My parents had to listen after I went through my bedroom window, plate glass slicing through my skin

105

as her heart leapt after his passing motorcycle. I lay bleeding on the lawn, paramedics shielding me from my mother's frantic screams, my father's swearing. They peeled my fingers away from my shattered clarinet, spoke to each other over my slashed body. Blood pressure. Heart rate.

"It's not mine," I said.

"Yes, it's fine," the female medic said comfortingly.

"Not *mine*," I repeated. "My heart is not mine."

My mother's wail went up a notch, my father's epithets one degree warmer as the medics exchanged glances.

They put me on suicide watch though I tried to explain, the door to my hospital room firmly shut against raised voices in the hallway. The IV dripped and my eyes grew heavy, welcoming the fog of drugs to ease a heartbreak not my own.

Mom came to me in the night, her will not strong enough to go against Dad in the light of day. Her hand found mine and I struggled to consciousness, back to the pain that was now both within and without.

"Sasha," Mom said, her voice a gentle breath. Then more quietly, a question. "Shanna?"

My heart leapt at this strange name, as if it would beat through my chest into my mother's arms. My hand clenched on hers and she cried again, this time a silent weeping that devastated her body, shoulders wracked, face contorted. I wondered how I'd felt this phantom inside me only recently, not seeing her earlier in the perpetual dark circles under Mom's eyes, the long silences between my parents that had stretched further over the years.

"Shanna," I repeated, heavy lips awkward.

"She died early," Mom said, and my heart skipped a beat, as if in silent recognition of this truth. "The doctors said you absorbed her."

"Not all of her."

Dad pushed for a mental facility, threatening to put Mom in there with me if she persisted in encouraging my twisted fantasy. But there were others who listened, doctors whose beliefs included things unheard of. When they suggested mirror therapy I jumped at the chance, ready to attempt anything to ease the unhealable ache inside me, the continued yearning for a boy I did not care for.

The box had two mirrors in the center, perpendicular to each other. An amputee could put their stump in one side, their good arm in another, and trick the brain into believing that a fist clenched for years was finally letting go as the inverse image of the good hand relaxed. Feet were scratched, atrophied muscles stretched, burning sensations cooled. I expected nothing more than the side view of my own face, another dead end in the search for treatment of an unknown malady. But my sister saw her chance and came forward. The heart that was not mine stopped.

A face not quite my own looked back, brows lighter, cheekbones higher, eyes red from crying. Our gaze met and my fists clenched, unsure what to do. A life unlived stared back at me, one I ended by accident, a chance kick in the womb disconnecting her from the placenta. She was owed.

I touched my face and watched as she stroked her own, a small smile forming on gaunt lips.

"Hello, Shanna," I said.

Mindy McGinnis is a YA author who has worked in a high school library for thirteen years. Her debut, *Not a Drop to Drink*, a post-apocalyptic survival story set in a world with very little freshwater, has been optioned for film by Stephenie Meyer's Fickle Fish Films. The companion novel, *In a Handful of Dust* was released in 2014. Look for her Gothic historical thriller, *A Madness So Discreet* in October of 2015 from Katherine Tegen Books.

Want more? Find a Q&A with Mindy on page 252.

Reunion

Joelle Charbonneau

I HEAR HER VOICE A MOMENT BEFORE the door swings open. That familiar sound, low and loud with an edge of steel, has me turning to walk back down the sidewalk—away from the door—away from the memories. But I tell myself I can't run forever from the past and if I don't face it now I might never forgive myself. Then the door opens. She sees me and I know there is no going back.

She stands in the doorway dressed in a perfectly pressed light blue dress that hugs the ample chest I always thought I'd inherit. Her bottle blonde hair that she claims is natural is longer than it was ten months ago and curls softly around her face. Blue eyes blink at me. "Sabrina." My mother's eyes meet mine as a small sneer forms on pink lined lips. "I didn't believe you were actually coming. After all, it's been a while since we've seen you."

"Rose said Dad really wanted me to come."

If my sister hadn't begged me to make the trip, I wouldn't be standing here now. I've been staying at my aunt's place five hours away because I convinced everyone the school was the best in the state and I would have a better chance to get into a great college if I went there. I haven't been home since last year. It's amazing how many things people need volunteers for over school breaks. The excuse that volunteering will look good on college application is hard for anyone to argue against. And summer school is a no-brainer. Especially when you want to stay away from home, which I planned on doing until graduation and beyond. Only my sister begged and pleaded. She said that dad's birthday fell on Father's Day this year. That they were having a small party. That Dad was ill and the only gift he wanted for his birthday was to see me. Please come home for a visit.

So, here I stand.

My mother toys with the collar of her dress as she studies me. The large ring on her right hand sparkles with diamonds and sapphires that more than once have bitten into my flesh, drawing blood, leaving scars. "You're late. The party has already started."

"My bus was delayed." My fingers play with the satin ribbon on the box I hold in my hand as I wait to see whether she'll let me inside. If she refuses, I'll walk away

110

from what I came to do and be relieved. I'm not sure I can finish what I plan to start.

Voices laugh inside the house. I think I hear my sister's voice. She sounds healthy and happy. I hope that's true. It's hard to imagine anyone healthy and happy living here.

"Well, don't just stand there." My mother's painted mouth curls into a smile as she steps to the side to clear a path. "Get inside before you let the cool air out."

I walk across the threshold into memories of my childhood disguised as furniture, knickknacks and photographs. My stomach churns. My head spins. For a moment the shadows of the past threaten to overwhelm me. Then I feel my foot catch and I find myself sprawled on the hardwood floor.

Pain blooms deep in my right knee. My left wrist throbs as I push myself into a seated position.

Footsteps hurry down the hall toward me as I raise my eyes and look into the icy blue ones of my mother.

"Oh my God. Sabrina." My sister races into the living room and kneels next to me. Like Mom, Rose is wearing blue. Her blonde hair is styled almost identically to our mother's, which makes her look way older than thirteen. Two of our neighbors follow close behind her.

"Are you okay, dear?"

"You poor thing. Can I get you some ice?"

My sister snakes an arm around my shoulder and helps me stand as my mother reassures her friends, "Sabrina is fine. Just clumsy. You remember how many scrapes and broken bones she had as a little girl, don't you, Margie? I swear, I was forever having to cart her to the doctor. You'd have thought she'd have learned to be more careful now that she's sixteen."

"Seventeen." Last month. But Mom doesn't hear me or she pretends not to as she escorts the ladies toward the sounds of the party, leaving me alone with my sister.

"Are you okay?" Lines of worry crease my sister's face.

My knee is skinned. Purple bruises are already forming, but there is no blood. My mother was telling the truth about my childhood injuries if not the cause. All things considered, I got off easy.

"I'm fine," I say, smoothing the red dress over my hips, letting the anger I never allowed myself to feel as a child swell inside. Anger will keep me focused. "Mom just welcomed me home in typical fashion. How are you?"

Tears well in my sister's amber eyes, but she holds them back. Of course she does. We are trained well. This roof doesn't shelter crybabies. If I succeed today it will also be free of tyrants.

"I'm happy you're here." Rose glances down the hall. "Dad will be, too."

I spot my father's small gift on the floor against the wall and retrieve it. "How is he?"

Rose pauses. In the silence I hear the answer. Sick. Weak. Maybe dying. Unhappy, but never without a smile.

Always pretending nothing is wrong because to admit the problem and the cause is worse than the illusion of normalcy. Until two months ago, I hated him for it. Fathers should protect their daughters from monsters.

Then Rose called—Mother's favorite, the one that never had an arm broken for not finishing her broccoli— and told me what she'd learned and everything changed.

"He'll be better when he sees you." She tries to take the gold and white wrapped package from me, but I hold on tight. After a moment she shrugs and asks, "Are you ready?"

Yes.

No.

I bite the inside of my lip and taste blood. The pain reminds me of why I'm here. "Sure," I say, practicing a smile. "What do I have to lose?"

The answer is everything, but Rose doesn't need to know that. Calling me—telling me about what Mother has been doing to Dad—to her—took more courage than I have given my sister credit for. Setting things right is now up to me.

Rose chatters beside me as we walk through the short hallway toward the party. For a moment, I think about ducking into the bathroom, but I know I have to keep moving forward or I'll lose my courage. I will my feet forward into the large open space of the great room. The two neighbors I'd seen in the living room are now in the kitchen. A couple of guys I've known since I was little watch a large-screen television that is new since I went away to school. My father isn't talking about the game. Instead, he sits in his wheelchair looking out the window at the yard beyond.

Some people say parents can sense their own children when they walk into a room. Maybe that's true because the moment I step onto the carpet, his head turns. I'd convinced myself I was prepared for the tiredness. The gray pallor. The pain in his eyes

I was wrong.

Rose hadn't lied. My father is on the edge of the living.

My mother's shrill laugh rings from the kitchen and rakes up my spine as I cross the pale gray carpet and pass the wrapped gift to my father with a hug. His hand clasps mine and holds it tight. There is still strength there. That strength gives me hope he'll be able to use the gift he places in his lap as well as the other one I am resolved to give him. In the package is the name of a local doctor my aunt helped me research and the date and time of Dad's first appointment. If my sister is correct, a new doctor, a real doctor might be able to put life back into Dad's face. But only if he goes to the appointment.

My father watches my mother talking to her court of friends in the kitchen then turns to me and jokes that colleges better appreciate how much I'm giving up by going to summer school instead of coming home for break. I try to laugh, and tell him I'm doing my best to make all the colleges offer me full rides so he and

Mother have more money to party with. Our neighbor Mr. Brennan jokes that he wishes his daughter was that concerned about the future and tells Dad what a good job he did raising me.

Dad shakes his head and says, "Sabrina deserves all the credit. I didn't do a thing." Then he begins to cough—a violent hacking cough that shakes his entire body and stops my heart. Oh God. Dad.

After what seems like an eternity, the coughs finally subside. He smiles at me and I notice the white slip of a handkerchief he'd put against his mouth is now tinged with red.

"Sabrina," my mother's voice cuts sharp in the air. "Can't you see you're upsetting your father? Heaven knows he has enough problems without you adding to them. Come into the kitchen. Even if you can't make yourself useful at the very least you'll stay out of trouble."

I take a deep breath. Count to ten to keep the flare of temper from turning into flame.

I hug Dad again. His eyes fill with the tears I wish I could shed, and his hand holds my arm as if knowing what I am about to do. Gently, I pull away, straighten my shoulders and head for the kitchen.

A bunch of women sit around the rectangular kitchen table munching on cheese and crackers. My mother is standing at the counter arranging vegetables on a tray.

I walk over to take my place next to her. "What can I do to help, Mother?"

"I'd ask you to set out the silverware, but you know how you are with sharp objects." Mother sighs. "Sabrina had to get eighty-nine stitches after slicing her wrist open with one of my Wusthof knives. Always clumsy. How two daughters of mine could be so different . . ." She picks up the tray, takes a step toward the table and pitches forward as she connects with my foot.

God it feels good to watch her launch in the air. I didn't expect that surge of excitement. Perhaps there is more of the evil from this house in me than I want to believe. The tray flies from her hands as she lands on the beige ceramic tile with a thud. Red, orange, green and white edible confetti surround her.

Trying to look concerned, I hurry to her side. "Are you okay, Mother?"

My sister runs into the kitchen. Her eyes meet mine. Deep inside them I see understanding and maybe even a hint of applause. The women at the table babble their concern as Mother shakes off my hand and glares at me. "How dare you?"

My eyes widen with innocent dismay. "I'm just trying to help you get up, Mother, like you always helped me." My foot connects with her hip as I reach down again to assist her.

Her eyes burn with white hot rage. I don't move fast enough as she backhands me away and the sapphire and diamond ring catches the side of my hand and tears a line across my flesh.

116

I yelp even though in the past I've always kept silent. Compared to other wounds, this one is minor, but the others don't know that. Mrs. Kral hurries for a wet towel and is putting it on my hand. The other women try to say that my mother never meant to hurt me as she climbs to her feet.

"For heaven's sake, Sabrina just has a little cut. Nothing to make a fuss over." Her eyes glitter. Her hands tremble. I know she wants to do something that is worth making a fuss over. Good. I want her to try.

Right now she's upset and angry. I want her even angrier.

"You're right, Mother." I smile. "This is nothing compared to the time you pushed me down the stairs when I was ten. Head wounds are a lot messier."

My mother sucks in air. In the background, the television blares out "Take Me Out To The Ballgame." Straightening her shoulders, Mother says, "You fell down those stairs all by yourself and I was the one who had to clean up the mess."

She waits for me to back down as I always have. To admit my mistake. Well, not this time, Mom.

"I put on a pink shirt. You wanted me to wear the yellow one. When I wouldn't change you told me I'd be sorry. It only took one push at the top of the stairs for you to be right."

"God made you trip."

"God had nothing to do with it."

"You broke the commandment. You didn't honor your mother."

"You're not my mother."

There are gasps. Rose looks stunned. My mother's eyes widen. Then her mouth curls into a smile. "I wondered if you knew."

I hadn't then. Not until this year, while taking AP bio. We learned about genetics and had to fill out a sheet about our families and our blood types. It wasn't until I finished filling in the chart that I understood what it meant. And even then I double-checked to make sure I wasn't mistaken. But blood doesn't lie and I realized that the rules of science said I wasn't related to her. Only to him. And he'd let me pay for that while she had forgiven him. Of course, now I know she hadn't forgiven him anything. Both of us were punished. Only, I got away.

"It only made sense. Why else would you beat one child with a hairbrush and never raise your voice to the other? Why would you let one daughter snack on cookies before dinner and slice open the other daughter's wrist when she reached for an apple? "

"That can't be true," a woman behind me whispers.

My mother snarls. "Of course it isn't true. Rose, tell them."

Rose backs up against the black granite counter. Her face is white. Her eyes wide with uncertainty. My sister hates confrontation. She hides from violence. It's a wonder she's managed to survive in this house.

"Rose. Tell them," Mother yells. "Tell them now."

My sister stands there defiantly silent and my mother spins towards me. "You bitch."

"I think maybe we should leave," a woman says behind me.

"No one is leaving," my mother screams. "Not until Sabrina apologizes for ruining her father's party with her lies." Her entire body shakes. The look in her eyes is the one that I've been pushing for—the one that says she's ready to strike.

I slide my hand into my pocket and finger the small pistol I have hidden inside. Just one more verbal shove and my mother will attack. I can claim self-defense, although whoever defends me would have a hard time explaining the gun I borrowed from my boyfriend and brought to the house. Still. My mother's behavior will confuse things and I'm still a minor. Those things will work in my favor. I hope.

My mother stares at me. The silence stretches between us. She's waiting for me to cave as I always did in the past. She's going to have to wait a long time for that.

"You put laxatives in my food."

"You lie."

"You hid straight pins in my clothes."

"I never."

"You cut off all my hair when I was five years old."

Her eyes flash. "You did that to yourself, you ungrateful bitch. I took you in. I moved to this Godforsaken town to protect your father's reputation and this is the thanks I get? How could he think I'd forget that he wanted to leave me? That he wanted you and your whore of a mother? You weren't supposed to live. She didn't. You were supposed to join her in hell."

My hand shoots out without my realizing it. The crack of my palm against my mother's face sends her head whipping to the left and her body staggering backwards. Shocked cries ring out as my mother recovers her balance and charges. Her perfectly polished red nails rake across my face, biting into my skin, before her hands settle around my throat and squeeze.

Are the women around me trying to help pull my mother off? I'm certain they must be. But she's too strong. I buck against her hands as the pressure in my chest builds. My throat is on fire. The pain . . . there's so much pain as I fight to pull her hands away and fail. I'm going to fail. I can't fail. I kick as hard as I can. She yelps when my foot connects with her leg and her grip on my neck loosens. My sister shouts something as I shove my mother away from me. Mother's hands slip free of my throat and I reach into my pocket for the gun as she stumbles back into my sister.

For a moment everything goes still.

Then a drip of blood hits the floor.

Followed by another.

Mother gurgles. People scream. Above the chaos, I hear someone yell to call an ambulance as my mother slides to the tile floor. I watch her fall trying to make sense of what just happened. Then I look up and see my sister standing frozen in place with a bloody knife in her hands.

"Rose?" I whisper.

My sister starts to tremble.

"She was choking you." Her eyes swing from me to the other women who are looking at Rose with shock. "I grabbed the knife. I wanted to help—to tell her to stop. I never meant . . ." Rose looks down at Mom who moves her mouth as if begging for something. Only no words come out. A pool of blood seeps from underneath her once perfectly pressed blue dress and runs into the grout lines of the tile as people come running from other parts of the house.

A gentle pair of hands take the knife from Rose and hold her as she sobs. I hear a man talking on the phone to what has to be a 9-1-1 operator as I grab a towel and kneel down next to the only mother I have ever known to try and stop the bleeding. Mother taught me that it is always important to keep up appearances. So I put pressure on the wound. I try to help her. But there is so much blood and when someone pulls me away and tells me there is nothing more I can do, I am relieved.

On my knees stained red, I notice my father being wheeled to the edge of the kitchen. Everyone watches as he stares at the woman lying dead on the floor. The other present I meant to give him, but Rose mistakenly paid for instead.

Sirens sound. People rush to open the door for the paramedics, while others wheel my father back out of the fray. Rose sits at the kitchen table looking distraught and shattered. She could never have imagined this scene when she called me two months ago and begged me to come help her and Dad get free of Mother's iron rule.

I want to apologize for not being stronger. For not keeping the blood off her hands.

Then Rose turns her head. Her eyes meet mine as the kitchen fills with emergency workers. And she winks.

That's when I know.

She's her mother's daughter.

Joelle Charbonneau has performed in opera and musical theatre productions across Chicagoland. She now teaches private voice lessons and is the author of the New York Times and USA Today best-selling The Testing trilogy (*The Testing, Independent Study* and *Graduation Day*) as well as two adult mystery series. Her YA books have appeared on the Indie Next List, on the YALSA Top 10 books for 2014 as well as the YALSA Quick Picks for reluctant readers and state reading lists across the country. Her next standalone YA thriller, *Need*, will hit shelves November 3, 2015.

Want more? Find a Q&A with Joelle on page 254.

Not Fade Away

Geoffrey Girard

"Unterburnnnagown."

She tilts her head closer, like she does every time, forcing a polite smile. The other residents at this table are already cleared, waiting for someone to bring walkers or transport a wheelchair. "I'm sorry," she says. "What's that, Mr. Kurtz?"

"Therr goondaburnittudagrrownd."

"Is that right?" Beth still hasn't really heard him yet but his tone sounds like a declaration of some kind, and a reassuring "Is-That-Right" usually does the trick. It suggests she's listening, open to learning something new. Old people like that.

"All done, Mr. Kurtz?" she asks.

Mr. Kurtz looks away and waves his hand at the plate with an accompanying "Bah" straight out of

Ebenezer Scrooge. She freezes. Flushes. Almost four months at Heritage Springs and it still makes her nervous when they get angry. Always a jolt. Most of the time, they don't get, well, anything. Just kinda sit there. Waiting.

Beth quickly finishes clearing his area, shoving leftovers and utensils onto the plate in her hand, jamming Kurtz's now-empty one into the crook of her arm with the rest of the table's stack. The dining room is more than half clear, two nurse assistants shepherding the post-meal parade of shambling feet, aluminum walkers and wheelchairs out the double doors and into the adjoining area where the majority of residents will spend the balance of their evening.

She hovers in the kitchen some before going back for another round, hoping someone will first wheel Mr. Kurtz away. When they do, she tackles the last two tables, wipes down every surface, then hunkers in for an hour scrubbing dishes beside some middle-aged stoner named Benjie. The radio in the kitchen is on AM talk again.

After the dishes come the drinks. Little cups of water or juice. Most times, the residents shake their head no or ignore her completely, but she still has to go through the routine. Weave among their various seats and rockers and a dozen wheelchairs. "Would you like something to drink?" The TV on. Some terrible sitcom or cop show that none of them are really watching anyway. Mrs. Winhusen is staring out the window again. Mr. Ramey already asleep and snoring, teeth bared, hair-crammed nostrils spread and flapping. Mr. and Mrs. Schlueter have been propped on one of the couches beside each other. She's never seen either one speak, or anything, to the other. They could have just set anyone on that couch together.

The "Macbeth Sisters" are grouped up again, each in her wheelchair in a crude semicircle alongside an untuned piano. Mrs. Horst, Mrs. Wansik, and Mrs. Marklay. Wrapped in their favorite blankets. All wrinkles and white hair, each one older than the last. Probably weigh a hundred pounds combined and combined is how they do everything. So, they'd immediately reminded Beth of the three witches in that play.

"Would you like some juice, Mrs. Horst?"

The woman's eyes shift, stare into her in that certain way. Something Beth noticed right away even when she'd come for the job interview. Not just this woman. Lots of the residents. *Most* of the residents. The staring. Drawn to, she supposes, her "youth." Her future, maybe? Like wolves gaping at a sheep. Or vampires ogling blood.

"Yes, thank you, love," the woman says, reaching out a vein-knotted hand.

The whole room suddenly smells like too much perfume. Or pee. More like a combination, Beth decides, and can't shake this idea, this scent, as she passes the woman her cup and looks away. "Mrs. Wansik?"

The second woman does not return her attention, probably never will. Instead, her gaze is always ahead

125

at nothing, focusing on distant memories Beth can only guess at. Maybe better than guess. Even now, Mrs. Wansik strokes the baby doll in her lap. A monstrous looking thing with huge eyes, realistic toes and hands, and a dress with small polka dots. Oh, and a weird boy's haircut. Like early Beatles. All day, every day, the old woman sits and rocks and quietly hums tuneless melodies, stroking and cradling this doll. Whether she's lost a child or never had children or just likes petting dolls, Beth has no idea. No one else does either. Maybe the other Macbeth Sisters know, but how would you even ask such a thing?

"She's fine," the third woman says. "But, I'd like some water."

Beth pulls a cup off her tray and hands it to her, slow and steady. Mrs. Marklay's hands shake uncontrollably. Matching her twitchy face. This one long strand of silver hair sprouting off her chin like a cat's, wiggling with the little shudders. Close enough to touch.

Beth nods respectfully and moves away, working through the rest of the room for the remainder of the hour. More drinks. Resetting a musty blanket every now and again. Soon, she'll help the others get everyone up to their private rooms for the night. Stowed away again until breakfast at six am. She moves back toward the kitchen to prepare tonight's last round of juice and water, tonight's last awkward dance through the room.

Looking back, she notices the cluster near the piano is slightly bigger than usual. Three or four more

126

people. The piano is still silent. Mrs. Wansik hums and pets her baby doll. Mrs. Horst talks quietly beneath the humming. Nothing Beth can quite hear.

It makes Beth think about what Mr. Kurtz said earlier. What was it? The words turn and waggle, like jigsaw puzzle pieces tumbling together, then dropping into place.

He'd said: "They're going to burn it to the ground."

Beth brings them more juice.

She walks into her own house just after nine.

It's quiet. Or quiet enough, the constant drone of the TV audible even in the kitchen, a murmur over the whirr of the refrigerator, the nightly dishwasher run. On auto-pilot again, she drinks the last of the juice and finds some granola to snack on. Realizes she's staring at the stack of her parents' bills on the counter. The same stack from yesterday, and the day before. Today, big excitement, they've added a scribbled To-Do list on top of it all. PAY BILLS is just one of seven other things.

Turning, she heads into the living room where her parents sit on either end of the couch watching TV. Some terrible sitcom or talent show that neither is really watching anyway.

"How was work?" one of them asks.

"Fine."

In her room, Beth spends an hour finishing up some homework. Junior year is supposed to be the toughest, challenging, everyone says. If only that were true. Her iPod lays untouched on her desk. There's no playlist for a Tuesday night that is like every other Tuesday night. She scrolls through Snapchat, Instagram, Vine, then returns inane messages to friends interrupted finally by what has become her least favorite part of the day. Washing her face, brushing her teeth. No big deal, but every morning, every night, it's the same thing. Over and over. Another day down.

She rinses the water onto her face and looks up at the mirror. Tries picturing herself old again. Like them. Her mom. Her older sister. Or, especially like one of the Macbeth Sisters. So close to the end, they can almost touch it. Shaking hands and all.

It is easy to imagine. The water runs down her cheeks and chin creating unnatural ruts. The illusion of wrinkles and blots and creases. Also, she's discovered all she has to do is glare super intently at her own reflection, a staring contest that could go on forever, and she can will herself to, well, look older. The skin around her eyes steadily retreating. Her face growing more gaunt and hollow like an old Jack-o'-lantern. Her newly puckered cheeks holding up the deep sockets above. From seventeen to seventy just like that. Her eyes sunken in, darkening.

She keeps pushing the vision until only a haggard monster is staring back.

A haggard monster who looks just like Oma, actually. Her father's mom. The way *she'd* looked just before she'd died. She'd lived in an old folks' home, too, for almost ten years after Opa died of cancer, could only say the sound "*Nash*" for the final four years, and it was horrible, and endless, and even cruel. The family resemblance is obvious enough, looking in the mirror now. Just like that, and Beth doesn't see Oma, she sees herself. Herself old and frail. Alone and forgotten. Still waiting. Drooling apple juice from lips that can't quite keep the form of a smile anymore.

Seventy more years. She can't even imagine it.

Beth tries recalling the last time she felt more than they seem to feel. The residents. Her mom. Even her sister. More than just-getting-by.

And always remembers a sunny, green-bright day of blue skies and laughter. A little girl twirling and twirling until the sky became the grass and the grass the sky and how it all tumbled together, perfect in its hope and possibility.

She can hardly picture that little girl anymore.

Not like she can picture Oma.

Beth studies her imagined "old" self again, wonders for the first time if she could, should, push it a little further. She's always been curious. That superstition about looking at your reflection in the dark and seeing your own death. If she can see herself *old* so easily, what would she look like *dead*? Maybe just a flash of lying in her coffin, just before the lid is closed forever.

She reaches out blindly for the light switch. Her gaze still fixed on the now-familiar hag staring back at her. The room goes totally dark. At first, she sees only that darkness, but keeps focused ahead on the unseen mirror. The reflection and future waiting there for when her eyes finally adjust.

Then, something emerges slowly from the black. Like some creature crawling toward her from a great distance. Getting closer and closer.

Now, she sees it. This momentous reflection of death.

But it's nothing. It's only her regular face.

Shadowed and gray. But young again. The imagined old face gone.

It's just her again.

She stands like that for a long time.

The next day, Saturday, is a full eight-hour shift. Beth purposely seeks out an assignment involving Mr. Kurtz. Even volunteers to help change his pee-stained sheets.

Curious to know if he's still mad at her. If he even remembers.

And, also, mostly, curious to know who the "they" is. What exactly they're burning.

Beth knocks at his door before using the key, and someone says, "Come in."

The room smells of stale Old Spice and Lemon Pledge. Inside, Mr. Kurtz sits in his chair. His TV is on. He's watching some cable news show. His feet are up on a footrest and they are swollen and blotchy. A middle-aged woman sits in a chair placed awkwardly in the center of the room. Beth is pretty sure the woman is his daughter. Who else would it be?

"Can I help you?" his daughter asks, standing.

Beth shakes her head. She wishes his daughter would leave. But she doesn't.

While Beth changes the sheets, the daughter and Mr. Kurtz sit in the room watching TV. The daughter never says one word to him. There is a three-month schedule taped on the wall showing when the other two daughters are visiting. One a week, their names mostly alternating across the calendar. Some weeks are blank.

She's running out of things to do in the room, trying to outlast the daughter. She can tell the daughter is doing the same thing: waiting for Beth to leave. But first, it seems, needing to prove—to Beth, or Mr. Kurtz, or herself—that she's a good daughter, willing to put in the necessary time.

Beth gives up playing the game and heads back downstairs to start setting up for lunch.

Shortly, she notices Mr. Kurtz's daughter walking out the main entrance. She'd waited ten minutes. All in, a solid hour. More than most who visit.

While preparing the lunch trays, one of the other girls tells her about Tommy G., one of the night orderlies. He's been fired or on a leave-of-absence or something. No one knows for sure. But he'd gotten drunk or high the other night. He'd flat out yelled at Mr. Sattler, the facility manager. Was talking totally crazy, this other girl says. Making up stories about the residents. This other girl thinks it's all kinda funny.

During this gossip, Mrs. Gruber comes early to lunch again. Her whole mouth is bright red with lipstick. All over her upper lip and some even on her chin. She clutches a little purse against her chest with both hands. She does this every day, every meal. This other girl thinks this is also kinda funny.

The Macbeth Sisters arrive together. One of them takes Mrs. Gruber by the arm and guides her away until it's time for lunch.

Beth watches them. Then she clears tables.

A desolate hillside filled with scarecrows. Leaning together. Headpieces overflowing with straw. All different sizes. Several too tall, monstrous tall. Hunched over, arms dangling. Stick fingers as long as a whole person, stick fingers tapered into black talons which sway in the wind to scrape gently along the dirt, or lesser scarecrow, beneath. This goes on for miles. The sky above and behind them is the color/texture of TV static. In this strange light, some of the straw looks silver. Wiggling with little shudders. Close enough to touch as she steps into them. They are bunched too tightly together to pass easily without being brushed, and she feels the knotty and distorted limbs prodding her arms, her back. The coarse straw skimming her hair. Caressing her cheek. She presses farther up the hill. Closer, she sees many of the scarecrows are no bigger than she. Only a little straw peeking from beneath their newly-stuffed heads. She moves past them and the others, and eventually lifts, flies, up and then over the hill into the static sky. The view changes and now she realizes she is NOT the one escaping. Has never been. That is someone else, some other dream person who continues up and away from here. And she watches this other person go, escape. Unable to move. Unable even to scream. Because she has stitches for a mouth and a head of straw. Surrounded on all sides by leaning stiff forms and black talons. And still the other girl, no longer waiting, no longer trapped, continues up and up away from the hill and into the sky until she is just one of the little specks above . . .

Beth wakes up screaming. Not from the dream.

But because of what she's holding.

A baby doll.

Clutched tightly to her chest. One she had when she was a little girl. She doesn't even know where it came from. Thought it was in a box in the attic. Has no recollection of being up there. The next morning, she will check and find the box in the attic open. She'll put the doll back. That's the next morning.

Tonight, however, she pulls the doll close, gathers it tightly in both arms. She caresses the doll's hair with her fingers. Hums. Imagines having children of her own someday. Imagines them leaving like her sister did. Thinks about asking how their day was, and them lying: "Fine." Imagines them making calendars on when they might visit.

The feel of straw is somehow still against her neck. After many hours, she sleeps.

For a long time, Beth sits in her car looking across the parking lot at the sister facility next door where the "assisted-living" residents get to stay. They even get their own kitchens and bigger apartments. Yippee. She's heard rumors that venereal disease is a problem there. Eventually, the ones that don't die will come to Heritage Springs.

She is late to work for the first time ever.

Later, Beth finishes in the kitchen, shoving leftovers and utensils onto the plate in her hand, jamming the now-empty one into the crook of her arm with the rest of the stack. The dining room is more than half clear, two nurses shepherding the post-meal parade of shambling feet, aluminum walkers and wheelchairs out the double doors and into the adjoining open area where the majority of residents will spend the balance of their evening. She wipes every surface. Scrubs dishes. Half-listens to the radio on AM talk again, pretty sure she's heard this broadcast before. After the dishes, the drinks. Little cups of water or juice.

There is an even larger group tonight congregated around the Macbeth Sisters. Their whispers like wind in dry straw. Mrs. Wansik sits among them, caressing her baby doll. For a moment, Beth staggers, loses breath, thinks the woman is petting *her* doll from home. The one now resealed in its box. Then it is the hideous doll again, the Beatles-haircut doll.

She avoids them all evening. All of them. The nurses don't seem to notice. And none of the residents ask for a drink anyway.

Beth returns home just after nine. She tries really hard to ignore the whirr of the dishwasher. She stands in front of the fridge, can't find anything she's not already sick of. There's a new unopened stack of bills for her parents on the counter. A To-Do list only half crossed out.

When she heads to her room, one of them asks, "How was work?"

She enters the room slowly.

"Mr. Kurtz?"

He sits in his chair. The TV is on with no sound. She expects to see only static, the kind over hilltops. It looks like he's just staring at cable news again.

"Mr. Kurtz?" She pulls up a chair to sit right in front of him. Takes the remote and turns off the TV.

He stares beyond her. Eyes misty. His chubby little hand quivers against his chest.

"When?" she asks.

He looks at her for the first time. His eyes searching her whole face. Like a wolf pitying a sheep. Or a vampire enduring blood. Then his expression relaxes. His eyes shift downward.

A tear dribbles down his craggy red cheek.

She gently takes hold of his hand.

"Please," she says. "When?"

He looks up again, his eyes filled with sympathy. With understanding. And love.

Then he tells her.

When she arrives, they have already started.

All the building's lights are out. The first-floor windows are blushed faintly with gold and red. Framed within each, peculiar shadows stretch and frolic. She smells the smoke.

She swipes her card to enter the locked doors in front.

No one is at the front desk.

Some of the men have slipped the new orderly one hundred dollars to sneak out and buy them whisky and dirty magazines. The firetrucks will arrive before he returns.

The night-shift nurse, Carol-something, proved trickier. But not much. Some of the women have combined their various pills and slipped the mixture into Carol-something's nightly brew of coffee. Those who could then carried her out to her car to sleep safely until it was all over.

Beth moves slowly toward the main room.

Several smaller fires already burn in the back dining area. Two of the men walked several miles one night and bought two cans of gas, the night before the orderly was fired or put on leave or something. The same night several of the women took turns wandering half-naked through the halls. Distracting him for the needed hour.

Some of these same women are half-naked again tonight. Dancing near the piano, in front of the approaching flames. Like little children dancing in a sprinkler. Their bodies somehow golden and beautiful in the natural light. Sagging breasts and bellies jiggling freely. One of the Macbeth Sisters dances with them, Mrs. Marklay, her arms held high and wide as if conducting a grand ball. Swaying back and forth. Joyfully lifting one leg and then the next to a mysterious tune played by Mr. Cinquina. All four of the women are laughing. In the fluid light and shadows, it is almost as if none of them has wrinkles. Walkers and wheelchairs are pushed against the walls.

Mrs. Gruber's lips are red and glistening. Striking. Her purse clasped tightly. She smiles broadly and flirts with two of the men. The lipstick trickles red down her chin from the heat.

Mr. and Mrs. Schlueter sit together on the coach. Tonight, he clutches her in both arms, touches her hair, her head rested against his chest. Their eyes closed, smiling.

The smell of gasoline is everywhere.

Beth searches for Mr. Kurtz. It's harder now. The smoke filling this room also. She can hear the crackle of flame clearly, and watches as it snakes up the dining room walls and first tongues the ceiling. In ten minutes, the whole building will be consumed by flame.

Still, men and women stand together in clusters. Some helping others remain upright. Two of the men have stripped off their shirts and shadow box each other amidst slaps on the back and cheers of encouragement. *Their* breasts and bellies jiggling freely. One has a bloody nose and can't stop giggling. Another man, fully naked, Mr. Ramey she thinks, is attempting handstands in the center of the room. Women cackle and point, fall into each others' arms with laughter. Others are screaming. Not in agony, but for the fun of it. Some are simply clapping together. Two women playing pat-a-cake. Mrs. Quinn is singing loudly.

Cheap furniture dribbles flame like small balls of lava.

Beth coughs, the smoke burning her throat. She watches it curdle like waves across the ceiling. Flames creep into the main room. Every breath now an effort.

She finds Mr. Kurtz. He is standing near the other two Macbeth Sisters and a group of maybe four more residents. Most are holding hands. Mrs. Wansik is sharing her doll with Mr. Kurtz, who is talking excitedly and patting the doll. Beth thinks of his daughters.

Mrs. Horst spots Beth and steps slowly away from the group.

Beth freezes again. Like the night when Mr. Kurtz first told her of their plan. Because she's an intruder. Unwelcome. Unworthy. Seventeen. She has not earned this. Not yet. Not like they have. Not the same. And it's so hard to breathe.

Mrs. Horst steps closer. The flames burst and waver behind her.

She looks happy. Free. She looks perfect.

Their eyes meet, and there is compassion in the older woman's gaze. Compassion, understanding, welcome. Beth too afraid to turn away, and too determined not to.

Has already waited enough.

Mrs. Horst smiles, then lifts that vein-knotted hand to her. Beth takes hold and finds the hand warm and smooth. Strong. They move together back to the others. Several of them hold little juice cups filled with dark wine. One woman grins at her, smoking a big cigar.

Beth decisively thrusts out both her arms. Steps back.

Then she twirls and twirls. Until the sky becomes the grass and the grass the sky.

She is happy again. Free. She is perfect.

Surrounding her, there is more clapping, more laughter.

Then more flames.

Geoffrey Girard writes thrillers, historicals, dark fantasy, young adult novels, and short speculative fiction. First appearing in *Writers of the Future* in 2003, Geoffrey has since sold more than sixty short stories, including the *Tales Of . . .* series, a collection of original tales based on U.S. history and folklore. His novels include *Cain's Blood*, a techno thriller, and *Project Cain*, a Stoker–nominated

YA companion novel, both published by Simon & Schuster in 2013 and translated into several languages. Geoffrey graduated from Washington College with a literature degree and has an MA in Creative Writing from Miami University. He is the Department Chair of English at a private boys' school in Cincinnati.

Want more? Find a Q&A with Geoffrey on page 256.

Blàrach Bridge

Lydia Kang

THIS IS WHERE DOGS COME TO DIE.

It's midnight in April. Spring has baptized the earth with warm rain and everything smells of thawed soil. I've been waiting every night by the bridge for nearly a month, knowing that sooner or later, I'd see it happen. But I'm impatient.

One more night. Just one more, I tell myself, shivering. The damp air sinks into my jacket and jeans as I stoop in the moon shadows by Blàrach Bridge.

Blàrach is supposedly haunted. Like its overseas cousin, Overtoun Bridge in Scotland, it has a terrible, mysterious legacy. Dogs are inexplicably drawn to the stone structure and leap off the bridge to their deaths. Not stumble and fall, but leap. Not one dog, but fifty.

There has to be a reason. After all, I don't believe in ghosts, or God.

I, Deven Bhatti, believe in hallucinations and terminal velocities; in rabies and psychotic brains.

There are far more frightening things, real things. And there are others, too. Like high school and empty lunch tables. I'd moved to Saoirse, Indiana, only a few months ago, and so far my best friends are still the library and the bathroom. I suspect even they barely tolerate me.

A mystery is a far better companion. It asks a lot of me, and in return, reveals small gifts of occasional truths. I fool my mom into thinking this will sparkle on a college application. Anyway, *Science Project* is more socially acceptable than stalking doomed dogs.

So here I am, squatting by this one-hundred-fifty-year-old bridge. As I massage my cramping calves, statistics run through my mind. Ten dogs have reportedly died at Blàrach Bridge in the last year. One rare witness said that a dog survived the hundred-foot fall, then ran right back up to the bridge, only to leap again, just like they had at Overtoun. It jumped and jumped, until it was too broken to jump again.

Just when my toes start to cramp up, I hear the noise. It's the sound of leaves and twigs crunching, slow and steady, like footsteps. I perk up and blink under the pale moonlight, searching. And then I see them.

There are two dogs. No collars or leashes, so they must be strays. Both are tall enough to reach my thigh, with long snouts and unkempt fur matted with burrs. One is dun gray, and the other black, with a few white spots. The two animals walk shoulder to shoulder and approach the bridge.

I hold my camera steady. As soon as my finger hits the record button, the gray dog's head snaps up and stares right at me. I shiver. The dog's eyes are big and black, penetrating and steady. They aren't the eyes of a rabid animal.

And then, as quickly as it had snapped its head up at me, it drops it again, as if weighed down by a thousand pounds. The spotted dog seems just as tired and worn out. Maybe they're sick? They touch noses, and stride forward to the center of the bridge.

This is it, this is it, I chant in my head. I grip the camera hard. The spotted dog lifts its nose, sniffing the cold midnight air, and takes off.

It makes two leaping bounds, one towards the edge of the bridge, and a cantering jump over the wide, moss-covered wall.

It's gone.

A gasp escapes my throat. *Holy shit!* I can't believe what I've seen.

For a long, agonizing second, there is silence as I wait for the inevitable. And then it arrives—the crashing sound of a body against the sharp rocks below, combined with a broken yelp, forced from the dog's body by the impact. I see it all in my mind's eye. The sprawling, lithe carcass. The neck askew. New blood and soft brains pooling where the furry skull has cracked open, egg-like, on the boulders.

I let the camera dangle around my neck, standing up abruptly. I don't know if it's still recording—if so, it's now getting a fantastic shot of my muddy sneakers. The other dog stands right in the center of the bridge. It doesn't seem to notice me anymore. Its snout points upwards, into the wind. I wonder if it can smell the death of its companion. I wonder if death smells irresistible.

The dog takes one step towards the side of the bridge. But when it crouches to spring over the side, I thrust my hands out.

"*Don't!*" I yell.

The dog startles as it jumps. Instead of leaping into the ravine, it lands right on the foot-wide wall of stone that curves on either side of the bridge.

It freezes.

I freeze.

But when I don't speak or move, it lifts one paw to move closer to the edge.

"I said don't," I command. It cocks its head at the sound of my voice. Once again, it stops moving.

It's working! So I do something really, idiotically stupid. I move closer and closer. The dog whines, and when I put my hand on the wall, the tail moves twice. Two little wags. I get up onto the wall, carefully balancing on the broad surface and trying not to look down. I hold out my palm and it steps closer to sniff gingerly.

I smile. And then it attacks.

144

The dog springs straight at my neck and slams into my shoulders. I fall backwards on the bridge parapet, my left leg dangling into the ravine, skull slamming on the stone and showering my vision with yellow and white fireworks. I cross my wrists to block the teeth from gnashing my face, panicked that I'll fall off the bridge and be smashed into smithereens.

The dog aims for my neck but only gets a mouthful of camera strap. It yanks and shakes its head viciously, pulling me closer to the edge. I dig my fingers around the strap, feeling sticky wetness were the nylon cuts into my skin, and drag it over my head to release myself. My center of balance is off, and I feel myself tumbling down—but miracle of miracles, I land on the bridge side, not the ravine. I'm panting and frantic. The dog stands on the parapet just above me, camera hanging from its mouth, foam dripping from its teeth.

And then it drops its quarry into the ravine. Distantly, I hear plastic and metal shattering on the rocks below. The last thing I see is the dog shooting back towards the road, running at full speed away from Blàrach Bridge, its shadowy form consumed by the darkness.

I run home. I know what happens in horror movies. I was supposed to go exploring a slippery, ink-black ravine to retrieve my camera. I'd end up tripping over a dead dog and waking up whatever was down there luring them to their deaths.

I may be curious, but I'm not stupid.

My house is across the bridge in a housing development that boasts a gravel road and a row of dead pine trees for landscaping. I open the door without a creak. Mom's asleep in an armchair, wrapped up in the same fake silk robe she's had for years. It barely covers her wrists. I peel off my muddy shoes by the front door and tiptoe past the living room to the bottom of the stairs.

"Only a crazy mother would let her only son wander around at night alone." Her eyes are still closed.

"Hi, Mom." I walk over and kiss her on the cheek, and she slaps mine in return, as gentle and loving as a slap can be.

"If this gets you into Harvard, then good. If it doesn't, I won't make you steamed *modak* anymore."

"That sounds fair, as long as you still make me *gulabjamun*." Which is actually my favorite dessert. I pretend that *modak* is, for bargaining purposes. Shit, I just gave that away, didn't I?

She waves her hand at me. "Look at this mud! Did you tumble into that new construction site? And why do you care so much about dead dogs? Aren't living people good enough for you?"

I paused. They may be good enough for me. It's just I'm not good enough for them. I never have been. I sigh and she sighs, because we both know the answer.

"Good night, Mom."

"You drive me crazy. Good night, my little Deven."

There is a thread of fear in her voice, in her wishing me good. A good night, a good day, a good appetite. Dark things always lurk on the edge of my existence, and Mom felt this since my birth. Her son came out backwards, on the wrong day, with the wrong doctor, at the wrong hospital, and on the wrong continent. When the first contraction came, my father called for the doctor, went out for cigarettes, and never returned. She says that hounds in the distance howled the moment her water broke. In my dreams, they still howl. But I don't tell her this.

I put on some clean sweats and climb into bed. Moonlight still glows in the night sky, but darkness continues to nip at the edge of my life in this new home. I think of my broken camera, and the dog that didn't die. I wonder if the dead dog is happy, and if the living one mourns its stolen fate.

Blàrach Bridge is still calling for me.

I go to sleep with my eyes wide open.

The next day is Saturday. I don't wake up until almost midday, and by the time I manage to finish my chores, it's late afternoon. I yank on my mud-crusted sneakers and trot back to the bridge.

It's a cloudy day, the kind where the sky resembles matted felt. A thin fog hugs the ground and tangles around my legs as I walk. When I reach down to scoop up a handful, the same thing always happens. My cupped palm is empty. There's a lesson in that, but I'm not sure what.

The brooding wood comes up quickly, still spindly with new leaves. Just beyond, the sound of trickling water welcomes me. This will be quick. I'll climb down to the small ravine, find my camera, and go home. Maybe it isn't completely broken. Maybe the recording of the first dog jump is still intact. If so, it would be the first video documentation of a dog suicide on the bridge. Ever. But something drives me beyond owning the bragging rights of first documentation.

I have to know the truth.

I've been obsessed with Overtoun for years. Dueling sensations of horror and comfort melted over me when I'd first read about it. Stashed beneath my bed is a secretly saved roll of money for a trip to Scotland. After my mother's job moved us to Saoirse (I'd pointed out that it had the best public school system in the state), Blàrach took Overtoun's place in my heart.

When Mom sends me to get the mail from the communal box down the road, I'd find myself at the bridge and not realize I'd daydream-walked an extra half-mile. I nap constantly so I'll have the energy to stay up all night. I live in the library during my free time, researching animal suicides. For me, there is no alternative to knowing the truth.

No one else comes to Blàrach. So when I go to retrieve my camera, I'm shocked to see someone there.

On my bridge, looking right over the edge where I'd lost my camera.

She's about my age, perhaps an inch shorter. Her hair is light brown, hanging loosely and shading her features. A threadbare T-shirt clings to her angular shoulders. She wears an uneven, black skirt. I can't tell if the hem is torn on purpose or not. She holds a pair of sandals in her right hand, and her feet look sturdy. She looks like the kind of person who holds the best kind of secrets, and would share them if you were special enough.

But I cringe at the sight of her. I don't want to talk to anyone, or explain why I'm here. Hopefully the girl will leave when she sees me. Most people my age in Saoirse tend to exit out of my orbit after a few seconds.

So I plant myself about four feet away from her and stare over the edge too. A minute goes by. Then two more. The silence is slightly more comfortable than nails on a chalkboard.

She doesn't move.

Three more minutes. I'm dying inside. Why won't she leave?

I cough, loudly enough to spew pretend rhinovirus all over anyone in my proximity. It's a threat. I cough again, trying to pull up some imaginary phlegm from my throat.

"That's the fakest cough I've ever heard," she notes. She has a slight accent. Scottish? Irish?

"Uh. Thanks."

"Is that your camera down there?" She points with a long finger. Her nails are dirty.

I hesitate. This is the longest conversation I'd had with anyone besides my mom in a month. The librarians don't count. My own internal monologues don't either.

"Yes," I admit.

"Well, you'd better get it. It's going to rain later and it'll wash downstream."

"Why are you here?" I ask.

"That's a very rude question," she said.

My face flushes hotly, conceding her point. She turns to me. I can see her face now, under all the brown hair. Her eyes are large and green, and she has Cupid's bow lips.

"I'll get it for you," she offers.

"No! No, it's okay. I'll get it."

She peers at me closer. "How'd you lose it?"

"I'd rather not say," I mumble.

"Were you taking naked pictures of yourself?"

"God, no!" I blush harder, which does not help my defense.

She clearly isn't leaving. What if she hopes to steal my camera? I don't recognize her from school. There'd be no way to track her down. So I shrug my shoulders and walk around the bridge, making my way down to the stream.

It's steep, slippery, and smells of skunk cabbage. I've never actually been down here and the humid stillness makes the hair on the back of my neck rise. Jackin-the-pulpits sprout all over the place, and brambles from raspberry bushes catch on my sleeves. The sound of the water is a relentless rushing in my head. I'm halfway down when the girl speaks almost in my ear.

"It would be easier if we had a rope to get back up."

She's right behind me. I didn't even realize she'd followed me down. Her skirt is hiked up and she tucked the hem into her waistband, allowing her long legs to glow like pale sticks in the gloom. The thorn bushes have scratched red marks onto her skin in a few places, but she seems unaffected. She still has no shoes on.

"Um, I can do this by myself," I tell her.

"I know."

I huff, exasperated.

We reach the bottom of the ravine, and I remember where I am. There ought to be a dead dog down here along with my camera. It's godawful dark, and the cloudy day doesn't help.

A shiny piece of silver plastic catches my eye. Wedged between two nearby rocks, it's the same kind as on the casing of my camera. The dark water ripples on either side of the rocks, and a deep pool of water gurgles behind them.

There it is. The camera is mostly in once piece, but it's underwater. My heart sinks. There's no way it will be salvageable, but maybe the memory card will still work if I dry it out. I push my sleeve up and reach into the icy water. I grab the cracked camera, but the strap is tethered on something.

I tug, and tug again. It's snagged on a submerged branch. I pull again with a grunt, and this time bring the branch up, with the strap tangled around it stubbornly.

My mouth drops open in a silent gasp.

It's not a branch. The strap is tangled on a rotting, human arm.

"Shit, *shit*, oh my God!" I scream. I drop the camera and scramble backwards, tripping and landing in the water. The stream is swollen with recent rain and strong. Cold water forces its way into my clothes against my skin, drenching me.

And then I see them all. Bones, littering the stream beneath me. Human bones. Skulls. With a blurred eye, they seem like strewn branches fallen from trees. But now I can see that some still have tattered bits of purpling, decayed flesh on them. The putrid smell in the air isn't skunk cabbage. It's rotting bodies.

"Oh my God. Are you seeing what I'm seeing?" I ask out loud, voice shaking. When no one answers me, I turn around.

The girl is gone.

I climb out of the ravine and run all the way home, eyes wild with fear. I don't have a phone. Mom thinks that phones are a means by which evil people might grab hold of my tender soul and corrupt me (she is fine with me hanging out in the paranormal section of the library though) so I have to run all the way home before I can call the police.

Mom is skeptical, rather than alarmed.

"What are you talking about? This is a safe town. Saoirse never has crime. People here die of diabetes, not murder. That's why we moved here. So I could die in peace with a full belly."

I call the police, despite her disbelief. The police will only come to an address, so they find me here before I lead them to the bridge. They send only two officers, probably to see if I'm full of shit or not. Having police in the house in close proximity to her only son makes my mother go slightly berserk. She gives them an earful before we set off, the sun setting behind the treetops.

"Deven is a good child! Straight A's! That hairstyle is my fault. I save twenty dollars cutting it myself, but my shears are very, very dull."

"Mom—"

"Deven is going to Harvard, just so you know."

"Ma—"

"Oh, and when are you going to fix that pothole on Jefferson Street? Gave me a flat tire last month! I demand the city reimburse me!"

I just walk out the door and the officers follow so fast, you'd think they were trying to run. One takes notes while I chatter my answers along the way.

"How many bodies did you see?" he asks.

"I couldn't tell. Just a lot of bones. But it could have

been five? Maybe fifteen?" I realize I'm wringing my hands, and shove them into my pockets instead.

One says to the other, "No missing persons reports in a decade. Could be dropped from out of town." And then to me, "So there was another witness to these . . . bodies?"

"Yes. A girl. But I didn't know her. I didn't get her name." I wish I had, though. I don't say that part.

"And why were you there?"

"I was getting my camera. I . . . lost it there the day before."

"What were you taking pictures of?

"Uh. Um." *Don't say suicidal dogs.* "I was taking nature pictures," I explain.

"Naked pictures?" One of them scribbles this down dutifully in the notebook.

"No! No, pictures of nature. NATURE. N-A-T-U—"

"Okay, okay. Got it. Budding biologist, eh?"

I nod and walk on ahead, totally flustered. The officers chat with each other about the naked-teenage-selfie phenomenon. I pretend to wear a sheen of teenage innocence. I even start whistling, which is a travesty because I can't actually whistle. There's nothing more suspicious than a person trying not to be.

When we get to the bridge, we look over the edge. The sun has set by now and a twilight gloom invades the woods. It's too dark to see the water.

"We'll have to climb down for a better look," I explain, and the two officers exchange glances.

One of the officers holds my shoulder—his hand weighs a thousand pounds and my nerves fire all at once. I want to flee.

"You stay here. Officer Bradford will go down."

We peer over the edge and watch him in his dark uniform take almost the identical route down that I had with that girl. About halfway down, he flicks on a flashlight. We follow the oval of yellow light, but the brush covers the ground so much it's hard to see.

At the bottom, the light stops moving as he focuses on something. I wonder if, after all the quiet policing in Saoirse, this is shocking. He is a professional, though. Maybe it's as routine as buying toilet paper on sale.

The officer climbs back up. He finally arrives, sweating slightly and a little out of breath, and keeping the light on the ground where it won't burn out our retinas. His eyes go from the other cop to mine, then back again.

"So?" I ask.

"Well, that was something," he says. I'm impressed with how calm he his. He hands the flashlight to the other officer and retrieves a thick pad from his back pocket.

"Did you see them? Did you count? Was it ten bodies or more?" I ask, impatient.

He licks his thumb and flips the pages. "I'm writing you a citation for a false 911 call. It costs us money to address phony reports."

"What? Wait! I'm not lying! I saw it! That girl saw it too—"

155

"The girl whose name you don't know? The one who's conveniently not here?"

"But—"

"There are a couple of dead dogs down there, some pretty old. Probably a puppy mill from the next county over's been tossing their dead mutts here. This is not worth a 911 call."

"But it wasn't a dog! It was a person! People, I mean. There were human bones, I swear!"

The officer hands me a yellow citation, and serves me a frown that shuts me up.

"Harvard deserves better," he growls. The two cops walk away, cursing under the brightening stars.

No. It's real. I know it is! As soon as the officers are out of earshot, I stare over the edge.

"Looking for something?"

It's her. I hadn't even heard her approach. She must have been slinking in the shadows the whole time. My stomach curls, knowing she saw me make a fool out of myself.

"What are you doing here?" I demand. I'm still freaked out, but now I'm also pissed, hot, sweaty, and have a fine to pay. Oh, and I have to explain this to Mom. I don't care if this girl gets the brunt of my pissed-offedness.

"This is yours."

She holds out a tiny memory card chip.

I snatch it out of her hand. "Who are you?" I demand.

"Come to the bridge tomorrow," she says. She's still wearing the same clothes as last night. Is she homeless?

"Why?" I ask.

"Because after you see what's on that card, you won't be able to help yourself."

"What do you mean?" How does she know what I was trying to record, anyway? Did she watch it?

"It's what you always wanted to know. The answers. Overtoun? Now Blàrach? Come at midnight, tomorrow," she says softly. It's almost a coo. "I shall see you then."

"What if I don't want to come?"

She stares hard, as if she doesn't understand my question. "You don't really have a choice, Deven."

She departs back into the woods and instinct tells me not to follow. After a long while, I head back home, trying to process everything. It's not until I'm back in my room that I realize—I never told her my name.

I wait until eleven the next night to watch the video saved on the memory card, drying it out in a cup of uncooked rice. Not that I could watch earlier even if it worked. I spent the night before and all day Sunday in the figurative Bhatti Dog House, cleaning everything from top to bottom, including vacuuming dead spiders from behind the hot water heater. It was punishment for the $250 fine the police gave me. I'd never seen my mom so angry.

The memory card was still too wet yesterday, but it seems dry enough now. I cross my fingers that it'll work. Exhausted, I plug the card into the port of my laptop. The video app opens, and my finger shakes as I hit play.

I see the bridge in the pale light of the moon. The trees are rustling, and a crunching noise tells of when I'd shifted my weight from left foot to right.

You can hear me gasp, focusing on the middle of the bridge. The dogs are about to appear.

And then it's nothing but static. Grainy, gray and white static. Vaguely, I hear myself on the video cry out, "Don't!"

But there is nothing to see. The video is useless.

How could this be? It was like someone erased precisely what I set out to record. The girl must have destroyed it. Right? Maybe there was some sort of unexplainable interference from the bridge, or just water damage. All my evidence, gone. It's beyond upsetting. I shut the computer off, my body shaking and sweating as if I'd just caught food poisoning.

You don't really have a choice, Deven.

She knew I would see nothing. She knew I'd want to know why.

Midnight is approaching. I don't have to go. I could just go to sleep. I could forget all about the bridge. But when I lie down and shut my eyes, all I see is the curve of those keystones, the soft moss on the cracks, and the bones soaking in cold water. It calls to me.

The answers are there. It's time to go back.

* * *

No one is on the bridge when I step onto the mossy stones, but I'm a touch early. This time, I brought a flashlight. I have to go down and see what's there. I have to know I didn't imagine it all. Who murdered those people? Maybe there's a clue. This time, I'll bring back a skull or something, as proof.

I scuttle down the ravine quickly. The water is sloshing downstream, and it's far more slippery in the dark. But soon I see them. Criss-crossed white bones litter the water everywhere. Darkness hides the rot, but it can't hide the stench.

I seek out a cluster of bones in a shallow area, and bravely thrust my hand down to grasp a rounded white skull. When I pull it up, I try to keep my stomach from pitching dinner up.

"What the hell," I whisper.

It's a human skull, with the lower jaw missing. Dirty blond hair still clings to the cranium, and half the teeth have fallen out. The empty eye sockets stare back at me and I drop it, as if it's been poisoned by death.

This isn't what the officers saw.

"You still don't understand, do you?"

I jump at the girl's voice. She stands on the bank, her skirt twisting in the wind.

"What's going on?" I try not to yell. Am I hallucinating all this? "Is this some sick joke?"

She says nothing, only climbs back up to the bridge.

159

I chase her, but she's quicker and more sure-footed than I. Panting, I reach her in the center of the bridge.

"There are human bones there. I knew it."

She nods. "Aye." The moon is so full tonight that when the trees bow in the wind to let the light through, I can see her features clearly. Her pupils are huge.

"What is going on? The video was erased. Why didn't the police see anything? None of it makes sense."

"It doesn't make sense because you're using your brain too much. You have to stop thinking so hard, Deven."

I shout at her. "The police think I'm crazy. My mother is ready to ship me to India right now!"

"And yet, here you are. Again."

"Because I have to know! God, I don't even know who you are. I don't even know your name!"

The girl grabs my shirt with such unexpected force, I almost fall over. She yanks me close enough that my face is next to hers.

"Breathe me in," she orders.

Internally, I'm like, *Freak alert. Somebody save me.* But when she says to breathe, I don't really have a choice, since my body wants to hyperventilate. I inhale. She smells a bit like fresh mud, and faintly of the ocean and pinecones. When I exhale, she shoves me away.

"That's my name."

Okay. We have entered psychotic territory, and I am officially terrified.

"You're afraid of me," she notes.

160

I laugh hollowly. "I'm not afraid." But I back away slowly, anyway.

"Your scent cannot lie."

Run. Run fast, I think frantically, but I can't. The very stones of the bridge beneath me seem to hold me closer, as if I'm a ton of iron on a magnet the size of Jupiter. My heart pounds hard. If it weren't for my rib cage, it would have fled already without me.

The girl continues her approach. "You want to know why the dogs come here to die."

"I did, but suddenly I don't care so much."

"I care."

The girl springs forward so fast, I don't have time to react. She knocks me down and my back slams against stone. Her knee digs sharply into my gut, knocking the air out of me. Next thing I know, I'm neatly pinned down. I'm not a weakling and must be at least twenty pounds heavier, but she holds me with the force of a three hundred pound linebacker. I can barely move.

"Get off!" I yell, trying to unpin myself but getting nowhere. The girl's face changes, evolving from an expression of plain certainty, to sadness.

"I was sad to see you that night, Deven."

"What? I saw you in the afternoon. That other night, no one was here. Just the dogs."

"Just the dogs. Just the dogs," she echoed. "Do you know why they come here to die? Do you know why they seek out Overtoun? Only in death, do we no longer change. Only in death, do we go back to what we once were, after living both lives. Hounds. Humans. Back to peace. The bridges that bring death are enchanted. The unchangeable cannot see the human remains."

I don't understand what she's saying. My mind is whirling, and my blood has gone cold.

"Did you kill them?" I whisper.

"No," she says softly. I turn my head when she sniffs delicately around my face. "They killed themselves. There are few places where we can find solace, after so much sin."

"We? What are you talking about?"

"Your questions are too long," she murmurs. "You should be asking, simply, *What are you*?"

She dips her face forward, nuzzling my neck. My heart pounds, and I want to scream for it to slow down. My pulse throbs in my neck and temples. I try to yank my hands from her grip and kick her away. But it's like concrete has formed over my limbs.

"I am tired," her voice creaks in my ear, and moisture drips onto my cheek. She's crying. "Oh, my dear Deven, I'm so very tired. I have torn innocents to pieces. I have stolen babes from their cribs. I have been a slave to the moon for too long. I was ready to end it all, but then you called to me. Perhaps we both know I have one final task before I depart." She sits up again and looks at me sadly. "Tonight, I'll change for the last time. I will take my original form and jump to my final death. My soul will wash clean under Blàrach, once and for all. You want to understand. You want to know what I am."

I know what she is asking. Tears pour down my face now too, and there is a rift in my soul where she threatens to tear it in two. Could I say goodbye to my mother, to India, to Harvard, to human loneliness and a world of heartache? Somehow I know this is what I've been running toward my whole life. Dogs had howled for me when I entered the world, the day I was born. I can feel her nails turning to claws against my wrists, her canines lengthening against my neck.

I close my weeping eyes.

"No. I don't," I beg. "Please. I want to go home. My answer is no."

As the whites of her eyes are obliterated with yawning, black pupils, her voice lowers to a deep-throated growl.

"Oh, Deven. I wasn't asking you a question. You never had a choice." After her teeth sink into my cheek, rending my face through my bubbling screams, she gently licks my neck where hot blood scrolls down into my collarbone. "Just remember, perhaps a thousand years from now when your humanity finally awakens again. Come back to Blàrach. My bones will be waiting for you."

I scream again as she tears into me, my heart aching already—because I can't remember.

I can't remember why she's calling me Deven.

Lydia Kang is an author of young adult fiction, poetry, and narrative non-fiction. She graduated from Columbia University and New York University School of Medicine, and is a practicing physician who helps fellow writers achieve medical accuracy in fiction. Her debut YA novel, *Control* (Dial/Penguin), was a Top Pick by RT Book Reviews and a YALSA 2015 Quick Pick. The sequel, *Catalyst* (Kathy Dawson Books/Penguin), released March 2015.

Want more? Find a Q&A with Lydia on page 258.

Chasing the Sky

R.C. Lewis

T HE SKY, GREEN AND CLEAR AND SILENT, lured Akash through the groves of reed-trees as he sought a clearing with a better view. The best he usually had was from the roof of their building in the compound, but if he returned before gathering the assigned samples, Tanar Dev would send him back out with a kick to his hindquarters.

That was all right. Akash didn't want to go back any sooner than he had to. Despite the decent view overhead, the walls of the compound—the same walls, same buildings, nothing changing, *ever* . . . it suffocated something inside him and set it screaming at the same time.

Maybe today. Maybe the answer would be among these samples. Maybe after all these years—extending long before his own birth—they would find what they needed to expand their borders, or even better, start a new colony elsewhere on Pumilam.

Growth. Change. A different view. Akash longed for all of it. The longing pushed him as he chased the sky, farther than he was supposed to go. Certainly not the farthest he'd ever been. But far enough.

Too far from the compound walls when the alarm sounded.

Impossible. They were five days early.

Fine violet ash still filled the air when Akash arrived at the compound, coating the walls and beyond. Coating *everything* in its dusky, bruise-like hue, including his nose. As a little boy, he'd worried it was poison, that leaving it behind was the real attack. But no, his mother assured him, the ash was just a harmless, biodegradable residue from the explosions.

So many explosions.

The other colonists were only now emerging from the shelters, so Akash had the first look at the aftermath. The roof of the biology lab had nearly collapsed in one corner, with lesser damage to the infirmary next door. A grow-house had been completely destroyed—one of the older ones, fortunately. All that just from his limited vantage point. There was likely more further in the compound.

Everyone quickly fell into their post-attack routine, taking stock and organizing repairs. Everyone except Cinta.

"Akash!" She ran to him, her eyes skating from his head to his feet, taking in the thin layer of ash dusting him. "You weren't in one of the perimeter shelters?"

"No, I was too far when the alarms sounded. But I'm fine, Mother," he added before she could manage a rebuke. "I found some scrub to hide beneath."

His mind flashed to the mad scramble he'd made, desperate to find cover. Then the agonizing eternities of waiting, of hoping he hid well enough, not daring to look because if he didn't look he wouldn't be seen. A childish theory, but one he'd instinctively clung to.

And the buzzing that passed far overhead, the sound of every nightmare he'd ever had.

And another sound, a new one—an odd keening he'd never been able to hear from within the shelters. Almost music . . .

Akash wanted to ask about that sound, whether anyone had heard it before. Whether anyone had ever tried to record it because maybe it was the language of the Ioshee, and maybe if the computer could analyze and decode it, maybe if the colonists could actually *talk* to them—

"Did you get your samples, boy?"

Tanar Dev stood nearby, his arms crossed and the lines in his face deepening by the moment.

167

"Some," Akash answered, handing over his collector.

"Better than nothing. If the Ioshee have found a way to rebuild their supply of explosives more quickly, this research is more important than ever. Get over to that grow-house and clear the debris. Ratu can't do it all herself."

Little Ratu, several years younger but—thanks to the colony's strict population control measures—the only person anywhere close to Akash's age. He knew what that meant for their eventual future, but Ratu was still too young to understand. Her parents were not especially kind to her, nor were they decisively *un*kind, yet that hadn't quashed her naturally positive disposition. Akash and Ratu made an odd pair, but were friends nevertheless. So when Ratu smiled while trying to lift a broken support post into her cart, Akash smiled back and helped her.

Clearing debris didn't take much brainpower, allowing Akash's thoughts to return to the sounds he'd heard. Bits of code streamed through his mind, ways he might be able to tweak some linguistic algorithms he'd seen while wandering in the old database from Mulabaru. The first post-Earth colony had reached a high level of development before collapsing, so even their seemingly outdated information might be helpful. Maybe. But it would take more planning than that.

When the next attack came, Akash needed to be ready to collect a very different type of sample.

* * *

They were early again, but Akash was ready. He'd spent his days gathering and cataloging biological material without complaint because it kept him outside the compound, and he'd spent several nights modifying the hover-collectors he used to get samples from places he couldn't reach. To each tiny device he'd attached image and sound recorders.

So when the Ioshee came, Akash was away from the compound, as usual, but this time near enough the outermost shelter to get inside. No one else was there, as he'd expected—the other colonists typically kept close to the walls. After securing the door, he sat in the corner, pulled out his controller, and began piloting the hovers he'd left outside into position. Some he stationed near the compound, while others went farther out in the direction of the sensor tower that had triggered the alarm. Each image recorder's view filled a box on Akash's screen, and he could enlarge one or listen to its sound transmission by tapping on its box.

At first, there was nothing to see, nothing to hear. Then they came. So few, just four, yet the buzzing sounded like an army.

Akash carefully piloted the hover to track that group. He'd seen images of the Ioshee before, most of them from the early days of the Pumilam colony's founding, before the attacks began, so he knew what to expect. Their strange insectoid-but-not physiology, emphasized by the buzzing wings sprouting from their shoulders, but their faces too expressive to compare

169

to simple insects. The images hadn't conveyed how beautiful they were, their iridescent bodies shifting through shades of purple, green, blue in the sunlight.

Beautiful, but deadly.

Something else didn't match the old images, though. These Ioshee were so small. He maneuvered the hover for a better angle, just a little closer, until it registered the keening sound he'd noticed before. Not a sound, but a song. A sad one. And their faces . . .

Something pinched in Akash's chest. The Ioshee were children.

More of the hovers caught sight of the group as they approached the compound. The four of them gathered and pressed the palms of their spindly three-fingered hands to one another's before spreading out, high above the colony.

Something's missing.

The Ioshee reached their positions, and Akash realized what it was. They weren't carrying anything. No devices, no weapons, no explosives. Nothing.

Before Akash could puzzle it out, the song cut off. The four Ioshee angled themselves down into a sharp dive. Fast. Too fast. Their iridescent bodies changed, glowing white, as they careened toward the colony buildings.

"Stop, stop, pull up!" he shouted, knowing they couldn't hear him, wouldn't understand him if they did.

As the explosions rocked the compound, sending up plumes of the telltale purple ash, Akash had lunged into the shelter's makeshift washroom, retching.

The Ioshee attackers were children . . . the terrible keening a lament as they flew to their deaths.

No one listened.

Akash showed the recordings to Cinta, but his mother did little more than shrug. He showed them to Tanar Dev, but the colony leader just grumbled something about "Savages, what do you expect?" No one else cared, either.

Behind the words, Akash saw the truth. They'd all already known.

He couldn't accept it as they clearly had. Not when that song ran through his head day and night. Not when he watched Ratu playing with her imaginary friends. Surely no one would willfully send their children to their deaths like that, not even aliens. It didn't make sense.

No one in the colony could explain it to him, or even wanted to try. The song of the Ioshee echoed in his ears, pressing his insides to the edges of sanity, refusing to let him shrug it off. Not like the adults had. Only one thing would silence the song.

The next time Akash went out to collect samples, he had no intention of collecting. With extra food and water in his pack, and all the linguistic algorithms he could find loaded onto his data-tablet, he set off in the direction of the Ioshee settlement. Or at least, the direction the attackers—the *children*—had come from.

Beyond the last sensor tower, Akash found himself chasing new sky for a new reason. Not to escape, but to get answers. And maybe—if he was very, very lucky—to change things.

If the Ioshee didn't kill him on sight.

The reed-tree groves thinned and disappeared as the terrain turned rougher, mountains rising in the near distance. Akash didn't know how long it would take—no one had ever told him how far away the Ioshee lived—but he was prepared to hike for days if necessary, even knowing the kind of trouble he'd be in when he returned to the colony.

If he returned.

The looming mountains ahead presented choices along with a daunting challenge, but before he could form a plan, he heard it.

Buzzing.

Instinct screamed to move, get out of sight, but there was nowhere to go, and it didn't matter because he didn't want to hide. He wanted answers.

So Akash stood and waited as the buzzing overhead grew louder, his hand resting near the data-tablet clipped on his belt. It didn't take long to spot them. Two Ioshee approached. Not children—larger and darker, their iridescence muted. His heart thundered, every ounce of his willpower devoted to keeping his feet in place as the aliens descended. He braced himself for whatever was to come.

The Ioshee didn't land. In a perfectly coordinated maneuver, they swooped down, one to either side of him, each taking an arm in theirs as they passed and sweeping him from the ground. Again Akash fought his instincts, this time to keep himself from struggling because he did *not* want them to release him from the ever-increasing height, but he couldn't help crying out.

Back toward the mountains, covering distance and terrain in mere minutes that would've taken Akash hours, then into a canyon. His arms and shoulders burned, the wind stole his breath, and any remaining would've been lost to the view passing by. Yellow and orange ferns lined the cliffs to either side, small waterfalls breaking through now and then to feed the river winding along the canyon floor. A part of the world Akash had lived on his whole life and never seen because he'd never chased the sky far enough.

They turned into a side canyon, reaching a passage so narrow the Ioshee scarcely made it through without scraping their wings on the rock walls. Then everything opened up again, and Akash saw it.

The Ioshee village.

A sheer rock face rose above them, a thousand feet if it was an inch, with the Ioshee village carved into it. Akash had seen images of cliff dwellings before, mostly in the history files of Old Earth that the colonists had brought from Mulabaru. But not like this. Not with the glint and glitter of refined metal accenting everything, possibly reinforcing the structures. The juxtaposition of old and modern jarred Akash's senses. He couldn't tell how deep into the rock face the carvings went, but if there were walkways connecting the various rooms, he doubted anyone used them. The entire cliff was alive with Ioshee flying from one opening to another, some clinging to the rock like they were lounging in a favorite chair. The buzzing as they drew closer became chaotic enough that Akash wanted to cover his ears, but he couldn't.

It all passed by quickly as the Ioshee carrying him entered the largest opening at the center of the village and finally landed. Akash tried to stretch his aching arms and cover his ears at the same time and failed to adequately accomplish either. His eyes took in his surroundings quickly—a room carved into the stone, but with chairs and benches and a table made from combinations of stone, metal, and wood, and light coming both from the opening to the canyon and some type of sconces on the opposite wall.

Most importantly, though, they weren't alone. Another Ioshee sat waiting for them, large like the pair—the guards?—standing to either side of Akash, but different. Other than grabbing him and carrying him all this way, the guards had scarcely acknowledged he existed. The Ioshee before him, however, scrutinized him carefully.

Then she spoke. As far as Akash could make out over the buzzing outside, the Ioshee language was all vowels and sustained consonants melding into a carefully modulated hum. At her words, one of the guards went to the opening—the wall-that-wasn't—and passed a hand over a metal plate on the edge. A flicker, and the buzzing was gone.

An energy field to block out the noise. Much more advanced technology than he'd thought the aliens had.

The seated Ioshee continued speaking, and Akash reached for his data-tablet so he could start running the linguistic algorithms. One of the guards gripped his arm again, holding it immobile.

"But I need that to understand," Akash protested, then realized how ridiculous it was. "And for you to understand me, obviously."

"Unnecessary."

She spoke his language. Strangely, with certain sounds elongated in a way he wasn't used to, but she spoke it. Akash's shock gave her time to gesture to the guards. They left through a hole in the ceiling.

The adrenaline that had surged through him from the moment the guards picked him up finally dissolved. His legs shook. Everything did.

"Please. Sit."

His shaky legs took her suggestion as an outright directive, collapsing him into a nearby chair. "You—you speak—"

"My name is Iorren and yes, I learned your words long ago for better communication with your Tanar Dev."

"You communicate—?"

"Of course." Iorren tilted her head. As expressive as Ioshee faces were, the expressions they held didn't entirely translate. "What is your name, young one?"

"Akash."

"Why did you leave your borders, Akash? Does Tanar Dev have a message he could not send through the machines? It is not time. We cannot go any faster."

The words came through just fine, even with Iorren's odd style of speech, but Akash shook his head, confused. Maybe Tanar Dev had set up communication with the Ioshee to try to negotiate? But that last part about going faster, it didn't make sense.

Akash realized he wouldn't get answers unless he started asking his own questions.

"No, Tanar Dev doesn't know I'm here. I came to ask why you attack us when we've done nothing to you. Why you kill your own children to do it when it's so pointless—we've had the alarms since before I was born, we know the exact moment they're coming and no one gets hurt anymore. Why do you sacrifice children just to inconvenience us with a few days of cleanup and repair?"

Iorren's gaze intensified alongside Akash's words, drawing them out. "You do not know. You are a young one, new, so they have not told you."

Akash suspected there was much he hadn't been told, but could not begin to guess. The colonists had kept his knowledge as confined by the compound walls as little Ratu. "Told me what?"

"We do not 'attack.' Ioshee never attack. The children are ransom. If we do not pay, you will destroy all Ioshee with sky-fire, just as Tanar Dev destroyed our sister-city when your colony arrived. A price that destroys us regardless, only more slowly. Yet we pay, hoping if we endure, the horror of Tanar Dev's demands will one day end."

No. No, that was wrong and impossible and just *no*. Maybe all humans looked the same to the Ioshee. "Our first colonists had to be at least four generations before Tanar Dev. He wasn't here then."

"He was, and so was I. I remember. You are the first of your kind to be born on this world—your elders have been here always, from the beginning. They wish to live forever. That is why."

"That's why what?"

"That is why they require our children."

The purple ash.

Biodegradable residue. Harmless.

The guards had taken Akash back from the village, but deposited him well beyond the sensor towers so the alarms wouldn't trigger, leaving him with a long walk home. That was all right. He needed the time to process what Iorren had told him.

Among the many surprises, Akash had learned that his home, the colony, hadn't always been in its current location. The original colony was several miles west, near the Ioshee "sister-city" Iorren had mentioned.

The one Akash's people destroyed using sky-fire . . . a blast from the colony ship they kept in orbit as a support satellite.

All because an accident led to the colonists discovering a peculiar effect of the Ioshee remains, halting the effects of aging upon reaching adulthood. But only the self-combusted remains of their young, some kind of biological process violently turning them to ash. The purple ash infusing into the human cells.

The effect wearing off, requiring new infusions periodically. New offerings.

New deaths.

And now, the effect wasn't lasting as long as it used to. Tanar Dev was demanding the schedule be pushed up. The Ioshee were losing more children than ever and couldn't keep up the pace very long.

Before he'd left, Akash had promised to find a way to fix it. Somehow. A promise that prompted Iorren to give him one of their communicators, now stashed safely in his pocket.

As he walked home, he wondered how he would keep that promise. If he should or if he would have to.

It could all be a lie, but it didn't feel like it.

Akash's return to the compound was heralded by a chorus of rebukes, the entire colony in unison, it seemed. He'd been gone more than a full day and they had worried, understandably, so he took every rebuke in silence. Ratu was the only one who didn't yell or chide, just threw her arms around his waist in a fierce hug.

The force nearly knocked him over, he was so exhausted. He slept. He woke. And he went straight to Tanar Dev, ready to demand, to cajole, to threaten, to do whatever it took to convince him not to require any more sacrifices by the Ioshee.

The answer was no. The threats to tell others shrugged off.

Everyone else already knew. Everyone except Akash and Ratu.

"You're asking us to die."

That was Cinta's response, as though it explained everything. Akash glared at her—it was the only way he'd managed to make eye contact with her at all since his return from the Ioshee.

"Organisms eventually die," he countered. "It's a simple fact of biology."

"A fact for lesser life-forms which we have surpassed."

Not even a glare was enough anymore. "Only at the cost of Ioshee lives. They're *children*, Mother!"

"Do you care so much for the life of the food we harvest?"

He stopped arguing immediately. Not because her point was good, but because he saw she truly believed it. She thought no more of the Ioshee than she did a stalk of corn. He couldn't counter a belief like that with logic.

Cinta's eyes darkened. "Remember this, Akash. Without the Ioshee infusions, the years we've held off will catch up to us. That's how we lost a few of our original colonists several years ago, when they left the compound; that's why you were born. Most of us would be dead within a season, the rest in well under a year. All except you and little Ratu. All alone on a very hostile planet. So if a few dead Ioshee bother you that much, you can help by continuing to collect your samples, find us another organism on this planet that works as a replacement. Something more plentiful, something that will let us sustain more than this tiny colony."

Akash couldn't look at her anymore, couldn't find words for the revulsion cresting through him. So he didn't try. Words, even if any could be found, wouldn't fix this.

No one in the colony looked familiar. Hardness seeped out from behind the friendliest smiles, hinting at the ancient souls inside, clinging to lives they no longer had a right to. It didn't feel safe. It didn't feel like home. Not anymore. Not now that everything had changed.

Except Ratu. She was the same as she'd always been. She reminded Akash of the Ioshee children he'd glimpsed in the village, so playful, yet with worry

180

haunting away the innocence that should have been in their eyes.

Ratu deserved a better future. The Ioshee children deserved *a* future, any future.

Everyone thought Akash had returned to collecting samples as he was told, and he had . . . it just wasn't *all* he was collecting. And plenty of his collecting happened right inside the compound, in the oldest quarter. In the underground computer hub.

The one where he found an off-world communication link, through the orbiting colony ship.

They weren't the only humans left after the evacuation from Mulabaru. The woman on the other side of the link was proof of that. More importantly, they weren't supposed to settle on Pumilam because it already had intelligent indigenous life. The other evacuees had assumed Akash's people died in some accident en route to Dunyasi.

Tanar Dev had chosen to let that assumption stand, and Cinta and the others had agreed, because nothing on Dunyasi could compare to the resource they'd stumbled upon there on Pumilam.

Akash started making plans, but he had to work quickly. Especially once he sent word to Iorren *not* to send the next ransom, along with a promise there would be no sky-fire.

A promise Akash swore he would keep.

* * *

"Akash, what happened?"

He glanced up from the controls and found Ratu standing in the doorway to the command center. Not that the controls needed his staring—the computerized autopilot was doing just fine. Ratu, however, looked groggy despite how long she'd been out.

A little too heavy on that tranquilizer, maybe.

"There was an attack," he said. "A bad one. We're the only ones who made it out."

Tanar Dev's rage when he found the new lockouts on the colony ship computer . . .

"The Ioshee?"

"No. No, they were much worse than the Ioshee."

. . . Running through the reed-trees, carrying Ratu, Ioshee guards holding off pursuers with weapons they hadn't dared use in decades . . .

Ratu hobbled over to the pilot's seat, leaning heavily on Akash's shoulder when she got there, a sniff covering the slightest whimper. "The others? They're all dead?"

Or would be soon enough. Tanar Dev was already oldest and would go quickly once the ash wore off. The others would follow, wrinkles deepening before their eyes, bones becoming brittle, organs failing in short order. All of them . . . including Cinta . . .

"I'm sorry, Ratu." He put an arm around her, gave a squeeze when she sniffed again. "But we're safe."

. . . Reaching the perimeter "shelter"—in truth a still-operational emergency shuttle capable of reaching orbit . . .

182

"They can't get us here?" Ratu whispered. "Where are we?"

. . . Cinta's screams echoing . . .

"On the colony ship that brought us to Pumilam. We're going to rendezvous with people who'll take us to our new home."

"The colony ship? That red star we see at night? How'd we get there?"

Chasing green sky. Chasing forever.

Akash took a deep breath, the recycled air of the ship feeling fresher than anything he breathed on Pumilam. Freer.

"We chased the sky so far, we went right through it."

R.C. Lewis has taught math to teenagers for over ten years, including several where she found calculus is just as fun in American Sign Language. After a lifetime of thinking she didn't have an ounce of creativity, she realized she just needed to switch to metric. When she escapes the classroom, she writes geek-infused YA like *Stitching Snow* (2014) and *Spinning Starlight* (2015), both from Hyperion.

Want more? Find a Q&A with R.C. on page 260.

The Cowbird Egg

Phoebe North

Mommy and Daddy didn't notice the stranger's arrival. After all, the history was there. In the photographs that lined the staircase walls, a pair of infants was wrapped in their identical baby buntings. In the ultrasound that was still pinned to the fridge with a magnet shaped like a ladybug, two tiny boys curled round one another like shadows in love. To them, he had always been there, their blue-eyed boy, hair the color of the guts of a rhubarb pie. To them, their sons had always come in a matched, if contrasting, set.

But Davy noticed. That night, when the specter passed through and placed the other boy down in Davy's crib, he woke and screamed, edging to the far end of the thin mattress, pulling himself up the bars. His little mouth, frantic, twisted and he squeezed his fists through the wooden slats, groping toward his bedroom door for Mommy. She finally came, Bean snarling at her heels. She picked Davy up, rocked him, humming tunelessly for a moment. He closed his eyes, shielding himself from the nightmare—from the spirit child tucked inside his bed.

But then Mommy stopped, Davy still clutched to her chest, and reached down, caressing the other boy's cheek with the back of her manicured fingers. He let out a small baby yawn, mewling. The child was real, then.

Davy didn't cry after that. What good would it do? But he still trembled and turned his soft shoulder away when Mommy put him back down to sleep. He stared at his hands, at the mobile swinging overhead in the corner of his vision, at the enamel stars that dotted the headboard of his crib. Anywhere but at his brother.

The only other person who noticed the intrusion was Bean. He stopped at the doorway, letting out three decisive barks before Daddy called him away. Tail between his legs, he shimmied down the hall. When he got to Mommy and Daddy's room, he didn't lay on his bed in the corner. Instead, he climbed up on theirs, wedging his long dog body between their bodies, whimpering hot doggy breath against their faces.

So Bean knew too. But Bean was a dog. And of course Mommy and Daddy didn't believe him. They only pointed toward his bed, shouted "Bean, down!" and pulled the covers up over their heads.

* * *

Davy used his crayons to draw what he felt. Their house was nothing more than a blue skeleton made up of five indigo bones: two walls, floor, and steep, pointed roof. Inside was Mommy, hair yellow, like his; and Daddy, with a baseball cap shadowing the onyx eyes that they shared; and little Davy between them, holding both their hands; and Bean.

"Is that your brother?" Daddy asked, pointing to the four-legged creature in the drawing. Davy frowned, stabbing his index finger at the page.

"No!" he shouted, "Doggie!"

In the kitchen, hearing this, Mommy sighed.

"Oh, Davy," she said, leaning her weight against the jamb. "You know Bean lives with Grandpa Max now. Your brother is allergic."

"'llergic," the other boy agreed from the far end of the sofa. He'd stuffed a crayon into his fat-lipped mouth, drool coating his fingers and wrist. Davy narrowed his eyes, glaring as Daddy pressed a kiss into his brother's red, cow-licked locks.

"I'm you," his brother used to say on summer nights when they were put to bed early, when they stared at each other across the dark room, from twin bed to twin bed, bright blue eyes boring holes into blacker ones. "I'm you. I'm you. We came from the same place."

"No," Davy would whisper. "We're different."

To Davy, the small handful of years had only

186

made their differences clearer. His brother loved junk food, would tantrum in the supermarket for it. His cheeks were pale as the flesh of a peeled apple. His eyes were like blueberries pressed into batter. They watched him, unblinking—Davy was sure he'd never seen his brother blink.

"You're wrong," the brother said. Outside, the older children played in the dusk, calling to one another, catching fireflies. Inside, Davy wished his brother away. But the other boy just kept speaking in his flat, strange voice. "I'm you. You'll see someday. I'll take your place, and they won't even notice. They'll think we are the same person. That it's the way it's always been."

In the dim, curtain-scattered light, Davy stared at his brother. Under his covers, the other boy was stiff, unmoving. Unbreathing.

Davy made friends with some boys from down the street, the Sheltons, Matthew and Marty. Marty was the older, with braces and a plastic retainer over his teeth that made them look yellow, mossy. Matthew was two years younger and didn't speak so much as whine. Otherwise, the two boys were cut from the same cloth—black wiry hair; upturned noses; lean frames, much like Davy's.

They played in the woods out behind their house, where decades of boys on dirt bikes had worn down the paths to dust. In the winter they built forts from the gray-sludge snow that hardened to ice in the empty creek beds. On snow days Matthew and Marty showed up on the front porch, banging on the sheet metal screen with their fists until it trembled like hollow thunder. When Davy came to the door, his limbs were buried in the padding of his snowsuit; his ears were hidden under the flaps of his hunter's cap. The Sheltons would be underdressed, always, in their sweat pants and Kmart sneakers and knit hats, their olive-skinned faces and hands red from the cold.

Davy would race out to them, grinning, shouting once over his shoulder, "Mom, I'm going out!"

They would only make it so far as the end of the walk when the dreaded, the inevitable, would come. Mom's voice, calling back to him: "Take your brother!" And then the figure opened the screen door and came, tottering unsteadily, down the salted steps.

Matthew and Marty always rolled their eyes. They didn't like his brother for different reasons: he was slow, he wasn't funny, he always got hurt and then ratted on them. But they tolerated him so long as Davy did.

But on one steel-skied day, Davy decided he'd had enough. He stopped at the end of the walk and stooped over as his brother gripped the rusted porch rail. Davy riffled through the dusty snow with mitten-hands, found a rock, big as a softball, at the end of the path, one that weighted his fingers perfectly.

"We don't want you!" he shouted, and lobbed it at his brother. It was a fast, even pitch, and clipped the boy's brow before hitting the siding. Davy and the Sheltons watched as his brother took off his snow glove, lifting fingers to the welt that split his left eyebrow. Already the wound gushed. But not blood. Something white and viscous was burbling through his cut skin.

"Mom!" his brother cried, and turned back into the house, the door slamming shut behind him. Marty and Matthew exchanged one glance before taking off down the street together, their sneakers sinking into the powdery snow. Davy let out a sigh. He went to the steps, sat down, and watched as birds darted like sinister shadows through the blanched sky overhead.

Finally Dad appeared, pushing open the screen. "Are you going to apologize to your brother?" he asked. Davy sighed again, pulling off his cap. He followed his father inside.

His brother was in the kitchen, a blanket over his shoulders. The smell of rubbing alcohol was in the air. All that was left on his brow was a Band-Aid neatly pressed to his skin. He didn't lift his cornflower eyes at Davy's arrival—only dunked a fat marshmallow in his hot chocolate and sucked on the sopping end.

"Well?" Mom said, setting her hands on his brother's shoulders, her lips pressed into a grim smile.

He hadn't meant to hit him, Davy explained. He'd been aiming for the door. He thought it would be loud, that it would scare him, maybe, that it would be a good joke.

But Mom only folded her arms over her chest, her gaze hard, unforgiving. Below her, basking in her angry glow, his brother loudly slurped his hot chocolate.

That summer Grandpa Max finally agreed to help Davy build his tree house. He'd picked the biggest tree in the yard, the oak with the low hanging branches, imagining the nights he'd spend up there alone with the green-leafed boughs the only thing stopping him from touching the stars. His brother was utterly disinterested until their grandfather arrived, timber and tools and plywood sheets in hand. Then he ran out into the backyard, grinning through his heavy breath.

"I can help, too, right, Grandpa Max?"

"No," Davy said, but was overruled by Grandpa, who looked at the pair through black eyes narrowed, forcing a smile across his wrinkled face.

"Of course, kiddo." And then, for good measure, he shot Davy a look.

At least Bean understood. The old dog snarled when the red-headed boy passed, hackles raised. Good old Bean. His brother shouted "Bad dog! Bad dog!" But it did no good. Bean just tucked his ears back and lifted his lips, exposing yellow snaggle teeth.

"Take Bean inside," Grandpa Max commanded. Davy obeyed, hooking his fingers under the dog's collar, smoothing over the rumpled fur with his palm. Bean leaned in to the caress, whining.

When Davy returned alone, Grandpa was stooped over his redheaded grandson, steadying the hammer in his hands.

"Easy now," he said. Their fingers moved together to pound in the nail. "That's it. That's it."

"Grandpa Max," Davy said, watching his brother turn the hammer's clawed end toward Davy. His eyes became blue slits. He was taking aim. "Can I try?"

"Give your brother a turn first," Grandpa Max said. He reached out and tousled the other boy's cinnamon-heart hair, seemingly oblivious to the way he glowered up at Davy, waving the hammer at him in some sort of silent threat.

Davy and Marty found a cardboard box full of soggy magazines in the woods behind the Shelton's house. Dirty magazines. At first Davy wondered who had left them there. Was it a fairy? Some sort of porno fairy? But then Marty picked one up and Davy's questions were all obliterated in a rush of pink-white skin, candy red lips and nails, and breasts round as balloons.

Marty said he could keep one. Just one. Like he owned the lot of them, just because the box had been in *his* yard. Arms crossed, he stood over the box like Cerberus at the mouth of hell, immobile. So Davy didn't argue. The one he chose had a woman sprawled out on the edge of a pool in the centerfold. Her blond hair graced the tops of her bare nipples. The pool water formed a lake at the sloping center of her beautiful back. Davy tucked the magazine into the waistband of his jeans and pulled his t-shirt down over it. On the bike ride home, it became a magical talisman. It seemed to burn his flesh with its importance. At home, he tucked it under his pillow. All through dinner he imagined it there, luminescent in the dark bedroom, waiting for him.

That night, with shaking hands, he tented his sheets over his head and with one finger traced the shapes that marked the waterlogged pages like dark glyphs. His breathing sped. He glanced over the magazine's edge to the mountain of sheets in his brother's bed.

As if the shape knew it was being watched, a rustle of cellophane rose up through the darkness. His brother pulled the covers back, revealing a white face lit by torchlight, crumbs and spittle coating his chin. One hand clutched a box of Girl Scout cookies.

"Want one?" his brother offered, holding a wrinkly sheath of Tagalongs out over the space between their beds. Davy only grunted, turning over. He tried to hold the magazine close to him, but his brother's bright eyes were always open, always *watching*, so of course it did no good.

"Mom and Dad wouldn't be happy to know that you're reading that."

Pushing his lips out in a scowl, Davy shoved the magazine back beneath his pillow. "They'll only know if you snitch."

"Oh, I won't do that," his brother said, cradling the cookies next to his narrow body. Davy heard a great crinkle of sound. He wondered how many bags of Doritos, how many Pringles tubes and foil packets of fruit snacks were buried under the blankets with him. But no matter how much he ate, he never got any fatter. He had the same lean frame as Davy—was always stealing his favorite T-shirts, his lucky underwear. "No need to remind them about you. They're forgetting already—have you noticed? It won't be long now."

He hadn't noticed. But in a way, he had known. Lately, at dinner, when Davy talked about his day, his mother's vague smiles, her little "That's nice, dears" had given way to silence. Sometimes his father's black eyes would still flicker up at him and then over, to something beyond him, lurking past the dining room windows and out in the yard. Lately, he'd been feeling even thinner, invisible, even. He held his hand up to the dim illumination of his moonlit bedroom. Was it the light that made it look gray and insubstantial? Or was it because he'd all but turned translucent?

Davy clutched his arms around his stomach. He turned over in his bed while the nausea rocked him, cutting as a cake knife. Meanwhile, on the other side of the room, his brother snorted laughter through cookie crumbs.

There were moments in the years that followed that Davy swore must have been dreams. He'd come home to find all of his report cards scattered on the floor around the refrigerator, as if they'd suddenly grown too heavy for the magnets, or his image blotted out of all the pictures on the walls. Clutching a frame in hand— the school portrait with the laser background where the multicolored lights now arched around a blob of black ink—he wandered from room to room to room, calling for his parents, but no answer came. Finally, he heard his mother's voice in the kitchen.

"Would you like peanut butter and jelly? Or peanut butter and honey?"

Davy pressed his ear to the door, listening for his brother's chirruped answer: "Both!" As he leaned, the door swung on its hinges. That smell, that sweet acrid smell that seemed to be everywhere lately, wafted through.

"And root beer, too?" His father chuckled. "Oh, all right."

Davy stepped through the precipice of the kitchen, but no one seemed to notice his arrival. Mom was too busy cutting the crusts off his brother's sandwich; Dad was preoccupied with the ice cream sundae he was making for his other son. Green-bodied flies circled around the ceiling fan and alighted on his brother's jelly jar of soda. Even they ignored Davy. He set the picture down on the counter and stepped forward, his voice trembling.

"Mom? Dad? I'm home . . ."

But no one turned. Even his brother only flashed his pin-pricked eyes up for the briefest moment, then quickly away—as if Davy were something distasteful and best ignored.

"Who put this here?" Mom finally asked, brushing past Davy. She picked up the frame from the counter, wiping away the dust, caressing the image.

It had once held Davy, his pale hair combed straight. Now his brother—eyes twinkling as gum drops, hair the color of a handful of Red Hots—sat squarely in his place.

But it couldn't have been a dream, could it? Because they were in different classes at school, and he was sure that everything that happened *there* was real. He came in third in his class spelling bee. He kissed Lucie Henry under the jungle gym. He gave Marty Shelton a split lip for calling his mother a whore, then made up with him the next day so that Marty would give him half his lunch.

These memories stood out to him like rubies in a black cave—not just real but *hyper* real, sharp and cutting and true. When it started snowing in the middle of the afternoon, all the kids would rush from their seats to the window and their breath would fog up the panes of glass. It didn't even matter to him that, later, when the school shut down early, his parents never came to get him. As he sat in his teacher's car on that long, silent ride home, and felt the rear wheels fishtailing on the ice, and saw the headlights winking out through the strange blue twilight, his heart beat hard, and he knew that he existed.

That night, in the muffled silence of his room, he shivered beneath a single sheet. Sometimes, as he drifted in and out of shallow sleep, he felt sure that the room was buzzing with mosquitoes, circling beneath the still ceiling fan. But that didn't make sense, did it? Mosquitoes, in January? Sometime in the night the door opened then closed again. His brother came in with all their blankets draped over his shoulders and sat on the bed across from him. His sweet, sour stink followed him.

"Don't worry," he said. He reached into the pocket of his terry robe and pulled out a handful of peanut M&Ms, chewing on them thoughtfully. "It won't be long now."

Spring came, but this year all the yellow light and birdsong and crocus heads rang false to Davy. It was March when he started sleeping out in the tree house, still cold enough that he'd wake up all covered in tiny, jewel-like drops of dew. He thought that if he put some space between himself and the redheaded boy that he could stop it—stop it from spreading, stop himself from growing any thinner. But in April, when his hand shot up in class, Mrs. Zaratino's eyes still scanned the room.

"Anyone? Anyone?" she asked, then sighed and called on Tim Conway.

Davy lowered his hand and placed it on the faux-wood top of his desk. Maybe it was just a trick of the light, but he could swear that he saw the wood grain shadowing his skin.

A week later, in the golden hour of four o'clock he sat at the edge of his tree house, looking down and swinging his legs. A sort of strange silence had grown in his head, empty, but very loud. It had lulled him into a trance that was only broken when his brother appeared, hauling his considerable bulk up the ladder.

"You . . ." Davy said, squinting. But then he forgot what he was going to say. His brother pulled a Pixy Stik out from behind his ear and downed it, staining his mouth a putrid green.

"I'm going to need my sleeping bag," his brother said, leaning back and touching the plaid flannel with one knobby hand. "Marty asked me to sleep over."

"Marty . . ." Davy droned. And then something twisted in his chest, broke. He lurched forward, hooking his fingers into claws, brandishing his dirty, bitten-down nails. At first his brother only swatted him away. But Davy, clenching his teeth, pushed harder. He nearly fell. But he steadied himself and kicked and kicked and kicked. Pantry beetles swarmed his eyes. *It's not working,* he thought, then his brother opened his mouth and let out an alien, strangled cry. Davy heard the wood planks lurch, shifting. There was his brother—pale, teetering on the edge—then a thud and only oak branches, budding, shifting the light across his empty hands.

Davy looked out over the edge. The thing below was his brother. Then it was a body, the limbs splayed out at the wrong angles. Then it was something else. He scrambled down the ladder.

He approached it carefully, keeping his distance. Whatever it was, it reeked of compost, of garbage long left to rot in the high summer heat. He grabbed a branch from the ground and poked at it. It was gelatinous and multicolored—sickly, oozing greens; the ruddy brown of manure; and flecked with apple red and bright blue, too. Wrappers, Davy realized, turning a mound of what had to have once been flesh over with the stick's pointed end. His stomach seized at the sight of what he'd unearthed. A colony of maggots, their wormy soft bodies glistening pale white in the spring sunlight. Davy turned and retched against the oak tree's twisted roots.

"Davy? Are you all right?"

He looked up, wiping the bile from the corner of his mouth with his T-shirt. There was his mother on the back porch, her hands on her hips, her pretty lips pursed.

"I'm fine, Mom!" Davy called back. But his mother gave her head a slow, sad shake.

"No, you're not. Come inside."

Davy washed his hands in the kitchen sink. He scrubbed and he scrubbed with a dish sponge, but it seemed like they would never be clean. His mother watched him. There was something in her dark eyes—a question.

"What happened?" she asked. "Why are you crying?"

He lifted a hand to his dirty cheek. He hadn't realized that tears had started to pour down them. "I killed him," he said, and his voice was strange and flat.

At that, his mother only laughed. "Killed who?"

The water still rushing around his hands, Davy turned his head sharply up, peering past the kitchen curtains into the darkening yard. Hadn't there been someone there? Now there was only a vague circle of flattened clover, like someone had left a kiddie pool, filled up with hose water, in the shadow of his tree house, killing all the grass.

After midnight his mother checked in on him. Davy had been half sleeping; it hardly registered when she creaked open the door, letting a flood of hall light in. But then he remembered, and sat up, shielding the light from his eyes with one wrist.

"Mom!" he called before she could turn away. She stopped there, pushing her pale hair from her brow.

"Davy, you're up."

"Mom." He cast one hand to the far end of his room, pointing. "Why are there two beds?"

His mother looked. Her gaze seemed to pause, hiccup. But when she answered, her voice was smooth. "What? Davy, don't you want it anymore? You're not too old for sleepovers."

Davy stared at the X-Men sheets, at how they were tucked in tight beneath the footboard, how it was clear that the bed was rarely used. In the distance, a house cricket chirped.

Davy was amazed by how different his childhood home looked just before he left for college. The strange thing was that other than the few boxes he'd packed with posters and ramen and three-ringed binders, nothing had even been moved. His parents were different from the other kids' parents—they were in no hurry to get rid of him, or his stuff. His old room lay untouched as a shrine. But still Davy drifted through the rooms, wondering how he'd never noticed how small they were, or how crowded. It made him feel hollow, nostalgic. His father found him on the sofa at nearly three am, leafing through his baby book.

"What're you looking at, kiddo?" he asked, then sat down next to him. He touched one of the pictures. "Bean! You loved that dog . . ." Davy smiled, nodded, tried to push back the memory of those last visits to Grandpa's house before the old man went into the home.

Age had twisted the dog beyond recognition. He'd lifted the fur over his bony hackles, snarling at Davy. Like they hadn't once been allies. Like Davy couldn't be trusted.

"Yes," he said mechanically, "I loved him." He turned the pages backwards, past cut feathers of red baby hair. He and his father watched Davy grow smaller and smaller. Until he was a fat gummi bear of a baby.

"Now, that can't be right," his father grunted. He grabbed a slip of photo paper and held it up, as if the light, shining through it, would reveal the image to be false.

It was an ultrasound. Their last name was there, printed at the top. But the image was all wrong. In the murky, mottled space of his mother's body there were two dark figures: nascent Davy, and someone else. The two bodies were curled around one another like a pair of jellybeans.

"There must have been a mix-up at the doctor's office," Davy said, snatching the page away from his father's hand and tucking it back inside his book. As he closed the cover, he felt all at once angry and fiercely triumphant. But, for the life of him, he couldn't remember why. The only thing that came back was a hazy recollection of a smell—something rancid, and sickly sweet.

Phoebe North is the author of *Starglass* and *Starbreak*, available from Simon & Schuster Books for Young Readers. She lives in the Hudson Valley with her daughter, her husband, and her cat.

Want more? Find a Q&A with Phoebe on page 262.

Panic Room

Lenore Appelhans

Now

I'm, like, such a murderer.

Pow! The scruffy man falls backwards from the chain-link fence and into the muddy grass with a thump. My ribcage rattles and I lower my rifle. It's the one Daddy gave me for my sweet sixteenth, all wrapped up in a satiny pink bow. I can't pinpoint exactly when Daddy's motto went from the biblical *Thou Shalt Not Kill* to the survivalist *Kill or Be Killed*, but it might have been then.

This is not my first kill.

Joel and Bailey dash through the gate to drag the dead man away. Joel hefts him under his armpits, and the man's dirty shirt rides up. He's real skinny, this man. Daddy calls these ones grasshoppers. Because, you know, they played away the good times while all of us ants were working hard and stocking up on food to eat and water to drink and weapons to protect them both.

I've been assigned the role of sharpshooter ant. So, beware all ye grasshoppers.

Bailey grabs the man, the grasshopper, by his boots. Even from my perch on the roof I can see how totally worn out they are. His gross, blistered big toe pokes out of a massive hole. He must have lived through a lot, out there. Must have been desperate to climb our fence. But I can't afford to think about that now. In the war of us versus them, my job is to make sure we win.

Bailey might take the boots anyway. Waste not, want not and all that. Bailey is the unofficial cobbler around our commune, and he can repair almost anything leather. Boots, belts, saddles, and the red kitten heels I'm wearing right now. I don't know what they do with the grasshoppers I shoot. I don't ask.

If I don't ask, it's easier to pretend I'm still a good person.

I flick my gaze back to the horizon. Dusk is approaching and more grasshoppers might be out there, though if they are, they've heard the bang of my bullet, and they'll move on. No easy pickings here. There's another group, though, more dangerous. Those are called cockroaches. They're fat and greedy, and they'll take anything they can find, just because they can.

Sometimes I wonder if I'm a cockroach, too.

There's a cracking sound on the old wooden ladder behind me, the one you have to climb up from the attic to reach the roof. I twist around and see my younger brother Logan's towhead. "Hey, Melly," he says. "It's my turn for the watch."

"Sure you can handle it, Squirt?" I ask with a smirk. This is what I ask every time he comes to relieve me. I'm the best shot on the compound, and that annoys the bejesus out of Logan, pardon my pig Latin. Whenever someone brings it up, he challenges me to a one hundred meter dash, back between the barns, because he's fast like Flash. A track star in the making, as if any of that mattered anymore.

Once his waist is level with the roof, he hoists his leg and slides down the metal siding to our makeshift sniper nest. He taps my foot and makes his usual reply. "You know you can't wear those shoes up here."

I pucker up my lips and smack him a juicy air kiss. "Don't tell Daddy. Love you, Logan." I say it in a rush, but Logan understands I truly mean it. I click the safety into place and tuck my rifle onto its shelf in the gun locker and take off my heels to place them carefully into my backpack.

As I'm preparing to reach for the ladder, Logan says, "I heard a shot. Did you . . . ?"

I don't look at him, but I nod in answer to his unfinished question. Killing people bothers us both more than we let on.

"Sorry, Melly."

This is just the way things are now. Get used to it.

Then

I step out of Daddy's pick-up and my heels immediately sink into the mud. We're visiting the acreage Daddy bought with a couple of the deacons from church. It's flat and boring. Just a bunch of grass and trees in the middle of nowhere.

I must have a look of horror in my eyes, because Logan nudges me with his elbow. "It's great isn't it, Melly?" he says, as if his words could perform a miracle and make it so. Logan basically worships Daddy and thinks everything he does is A-OK. He's too young yet to be cynical is my best guess.

"What do you think, honey?" Daddy asks me when I don't answer. He's wearing his favorite bolo tie, with the bald eagle to match his bald eagle boots, and he's even tucked his shirt into his jeans. He means business, and the last thing he wants to hear is my real answer, which is something along the lines of, "Are you seriously freaking kidding me?"

And, okay, as much as he frustrates me with his weirdo ideas, I love him and I hate to disappoint him. "It's . . . really far out of the way."

"That's the whole point!" Daddy says. "More than one tank of gas away from the big city. There'll be less grasshoppers to deal with out here."

It takes every ounce of willpower I have not to roll my eyes. "Daddy . . ." I say, exasperated. "This is also more than one tank of gas away from all my friends."

"I know you feel like you're sacrificing a lot," Daddy says, frowning. "But keeping you and Logan safe is what matters now. I love you both more than anything. You don't want to stay with the grasshoppers."

He sets off towards the nearest copse of yellow poplars, with Logan happily in tow. I trudge behind him. He must take that as acquiescence, because he's Mr. Smileyface now. He points to our left. "This is where we'll build the house and the barns."

"Cool!" Logan exclaims.

"Cool" I mumble.

Daddy points at a path through the trees. "There's a pond down there, but the tree cover is so thick, you wouldn't know it unless somebody told you. We'll build an escape tunnel from the panic room in the basement of the house out to the pond. That's an extra chunk of change, but it's worth the peace of mind."

"Can we get a hovercraft, too?" I say.

He stops in his tracks, and turns to stare down at me. "You need to take this seriously, Melly. This country doesn't have much longer with all these morally bankrupt crooks in charge." He launches into his usual speech about how evil the political system is, and how we can't do anything to change it so we have to concentrate on prepping ourselves for doomsday. Daddy's number-one bet is that terrorists are going to hit us with an EMP to completely shut down our infrastructure, and that's all because "we're too gosh darn soft on those heathens."

I could recite this speech in my sleep, but I don't believe any of it. And I'd much rather be at the mall right now with Becks and Olivia. I slide out my phone to see if they've texted, but there not a single bar of reception. "Ugh! I can't even use my cellphone out here?"

Daddy nods, pleased as church picnic punch. "The government can't track us."

Tears prickle at my eyes. My social life is ruined, just because Daddy's all freaking delusional. I won't be able to text my friends anymore, and I'll never see them. I might as well be dead. "How far is the high school? Does the bus even come out here? Or do I get to drive?"

"No high school," Daddy says, like it's no big deal. "But we're going to set things up so you kids still get your book learning."

Homeschooling? I have to put a stop to this nonsense. "Daddy, but what about cheerleading and prom and National Honor Society?" There's an edge of hysteria to my voice as my dreams for the future are stripped from me one by one.

"What about staying alive? We won't be safe in the city much longer."

"But . . ." I start, but then I stop. It will do me absolutely no good to argue with him. He's set on this crazy plan, and he's going to bring all of us down with him.

A mini-van pulls up and out spring Deacon Fred and his spritely wife Sheila, followed by Deacon Joel and his meek wife Kathy—all here to oooh and aaah at a whole lot of nothing. Their weirdo son, Bailey, stays firmly planted in the backseat. I don't blame him. These are the people I could be stuck with for the rest of my boring, friendless existence.

Hello, compound living. Goodbye, everything else. Rah rah, sis boom bah.

Now

Before I go down to the Great Below, I stop by my former bedroom and trade my heels for my sneakers. I glance at my dead cellphone. It's still plugged into a wall socket that will never provide electricity again. I run my pinkie over my dresser and draw swirls into the dust, wishing, like I often do, that I could sleep up here again. That it wasn't too risky. My skin grazes against the tiara I wore as freshman princess as part of homecoming court. I loved wearing it, because it meant people liked me and that I had a bright future ahead. I fight the urge to pick it up and snap it in half. That night seems impossibly long ago, or like it's part of someone else's past, not mine.

I can't linger. Dinner starts soon, and I'm expected to help serve tonight. On a whim, I tuck the tiara into the top pocket of my backpack. Maybe I'll wear it to bed and feel hopeful again.

Standing in the basement, one could believe that nothing had changed drastically in the world outside. Oil lanterns hang from the four corners of the dining room, spilling their yellow light generously onto the long table, the sofa corner and the bookcases. It's frightening how coziness like this has the power to lull you into a false sense of security and well-being. I mean, cockroaches could crawl in while everyone's playing a rollicking game of doubles canasta and clobber us all to death.

I don an apron and head for the kitchen. Bailey is already here, back from wherever he took that dead grasshopper. He has a smear of chunky blood on his neck, and the sight of it turns my stomach.

"Ummm . . ." I say, pointing at the offending stain. "That's not up to food service code."

He raises one eyebrow and wipes his neck with a wet dishtowel, but he says nothing. It's not like he can't talk, but he vastly prefers not to. Especially not to me. Bailey is two years older than I am, and that makes him the only non-family, age-appropriate male on the commune. Great basis for instant romance, right? He must have thought so because a few months back, he asked to kiss me, and I was all like, "Yeah, Bailey, this is so not gonna happen." That probably hurt his feelings. But, come on. Bailey is into, like, wizards and stuff, and he wears black all the time.

While he stacks dishes, Bailey starts whistling a melancholy sort of tune, the type one might whistle at a funeral or a deathbed if one was inclined to whistle at all for such occasions. Not gonna lie, it's kinda soothing, and I find myself wanting to join in.

As I set the long table with silverware and napkins and listen to Bailey, I think of old Mrs. Hammaset, my piano teacher when I was a little girl, and the way she used to whistle along to my inept pounding at the keys, flapping her wax-paper hands like a metronome. She might have been approaching complete deafness, surely the only reason she took on a tragic mess like me on as a pupil, but she could keep a steady beat. Well, until the day she crumpled into a sack of bones while I was happily massacring "Twinkle, Twinkle, Little Star."

Mrs. Hammaset was the first dead person I ever saw, and of course I thought it was my fault. I was eight, so I didn't understand how people actually died, or that we're all made of a fragile system of organs and vessels that can betray us at any time they darn please. I had just stared at her, the sound of my own dissonance still ringing in my ears. Then I had shrieked until my throat burned. Mrs. Hammaset's trio of golden retrievers howled in response, and the neighbors called the police.

My parents consoled me with a trip to Ye Olde Ice Cream Parlor and a triple scoop cone. My child brain was convinced that they did it to honor each of one Mrs. Hammaset's now orphaned dogs. While I slurped and mint ice cream dribbled down my chin, my mom explained death to me and why Mrs. Hammaset's passing was part of the natural order.

I wish Mom were here now, to tell me the same about that scruffy man. But she's up in heaven, due to a freak brain aneurysm. And maybe that makes her a lucky sort of ant, because she made it out of here long before the great grasshopper scourge descended. Logan and I miss her, but Daddy took her death the hardest.

If you ask me, her dying is the reason he's so intent on us surviving.

Bailey stops whistling and starts into a droning hum. It's nothing but bleak. If he keeps on like this, I'm going to start wearing black, too.

THEN

"What are you going to put in your locker?" Logan asks me. We're early for the christening of the glorious new panic room, so it's just the two of us. I wrinkle my nose at the new car smell that permeates the cramped space. I'd much prefer a new car to this.

"That's for me to know, and you to find out hopefully never," I say cheerfully. Below the security monitors on the left wall, there are eight small lockers, one for each of the compound residents. Daddy's idea is that we all put something precious to us in the lockers. That's so, like, if the doggy doo-doo hits the fan and we're trapped down here like shelter mutts, we'll have some item that reminds us that life is worth living.

"I'm putting my first Bible in," Logan says. "The one Mom gave me."

"Excellent choice, Squirt, I commend you."

He smiles. "And a Spider-Man comic, too. Issue 661."

Truth is, I haven't decided which of my possessions I could stash in my locker to serve as my end-times nugget of hope.

"Maybe I'll put in a bottle of whiskey," I joke.

"Nah, you don't need to," Logan says. "Daddy has a whole case of it out in the bug-out bunker. He wouldn't let me taste it. He said it will be valuable for trading in a post-monetary economy."

I hate to hear Logan parroting Daddy's delusions. "That and because you are about eight years away from legal."

He sticks his tongue out at me. I stick mine out at him. Two can play at the brat game.

I walk over to the wall on the right and run my hands along the rows of generic canned food and bottled water. The white labels are crisp with clean black type, but look as sickly as the stomach flu under the fluorescent lights. I shiver, and squeeze my bare arms up and down until my goose bumps are gone.

"Daddy's thought of everything, hasn't he?" There's enough space and supplies down here for all eight of us to survive for a couple of months. There's a stack of mattresses, a hygiene station, lanterns and matches, and so much other crap. The set-up is similar in Daddy's hidden underground bunker near the pond, except for the whiskey situation.

I'll take the whiskey.

Now

Bailey gets a vase from the kitchen and places a bouquet of hot pink flowers on the table. They look like the ones that grow along the east fence.

"Special occasion?" I ask.

He ducks his head, but not before I see him blush. "It would have been my grandma's birthday today. Peonies were her favorite. My mom's been taking care of them in her honor."

His words stab something sweet at my heart, and I hesitate before I answer. "My mom loved roses."

He nods and we finish setting the table in silence. When we're done, Bailey looks at his watch. It's one of those old-wind up ones with mechanical components instead of electrical, so the EMP didn't kill it. "Where is everyone?" Bailey asks.

Just then, the special alarm that Daddy rigged up goes off and the room fills with sounds of empty tin cans crashing against one another.

My whole body goes cold, and it looks like Bailey's eyes might pop out of his head. For a few seconds neither of us move. I can't believe what I'm hearing.

But I clench my teeth, sling on my backpack, and grab Bailey's arm with one fist and an oil lantern with the other. "We have to get out of here!"

I pull him toward the secret passageway guarded by the Classics bookshelf, and then yank the fake edition of *Frankenstein* out to release the door. I shove Bailey through and hand him the lantern to hold. Then I push *Frankenstein* back into its slot and secure the door behind us, following the protocol that Daddy set up in case intruders breached our defenses.

We run down the passageway, and then I turn the dial of the panic room door's combination lock with shaky fingers. *Don't panic. Don't panic. Don't panic.*

"36-7-42," Bailey stage whispers.

"I know. I know."

Finally, the tumblers click into place and the door swings open. We're blasted by the mustiness of stale air, and we both cough.

Once we're inside and locked in, Bailey uses a footstool to hang the lantern on the ceiling hook where the fluorescent lights used to be. He begins to pace. Ten long strides forth. Ten long strides back. "What could've happened?" he asks, flailing his arms. And then he sits down on the footstool. "What if the others don't come? My mom and dad were just out by the fence. What if they're hurt? Or . . ." He shuts up and covers his mouth.

I stare at the useless bank of security monitors. Once upon a time, pre-EMP, we would've been able to keep up with compound current events via closed-circuit cameras. But now we're blind down here. And deaf, too, since we're encased in such thick concrete. I have no idea who is attacking us. I have no idea who is still able to fight back. I refuse to think about Daddy or Logan or Bailey's parents being dead though. That is simply not an option. "What time is it?"

Bailey checks his watch again. "7:05."

"Okay," I say. "We wait half an hour. And then we sneak out the exit."

214

LENORE APPELHANS

THEN

I can't believe it. Daddy was right. A whole month ago, at 7:21 am on October 2nd, an electromagnetic pulse hit us, or at least that's the going theory. Because everything with wiring or electrical components has been fried. Nothing with an on/off switch works now. Not my curling iron. Not the television. Not the refrigerator. I'm looking at potentially thousands of bad hair days, without ice cream, or contact with the outside world. And that's if the government is somehow able to mobilize and help us recover from this. Daddy doesn't see much chance of that happening.

There's not much to do for fun, unless you like skinning squirrels, and for the record, I don't. I have gotten real good at shooting though, and I can hit squirrels, even from pretty far away. Daddy's impressed with my aim.

No school either. Bailey graduated last year and Logan and I asked for a break from it. All the adults have been too busy since the EMP to teach us. Bailey's parents, Joel and Kathy, take care of the animals. Joel's a doctor, too. Fred and Sheila garden in the spring and summer, can in the fall, and do a bunch of other stuff in the winter. I don't know. I don't really keep track. Daddy manages everything.

We don't have any way to get news. Daddy had a radio in his Faraday cage, but when the EMP hit, the box wasn't sealed the right way or something and everything in there got fried too. Daddy was so angry he used the Lord's name in vain, and you know that's bad. No one has come or gone out of the compound since, on Daddy's orders. Daddy says he's sure the grasshoppers have eaten up everything in the city by now and they'll be heading our way, but since their cars don't work, it'll take them awhile.

Bailey says he thinks some locals are playing a trick on us, that they created some limited-range electric bomb and set it off outside our razor-wire fence. So we're, like, all in here acting like it's the end of the world as we know it, and everyone outside is fine. This would both fantastically cheese me off and be the greatest single thing ever.

Now

It's 7:10, and five minutes into our forced panic room cohabitation. Bailey raided his locker for a stuffed giraffe, and now he's sitting atop the stack of mattresses hugging it for dear life. It's kinda sad, but also, like, totally freaking adorable. I'm not such a scrooge that I can't give him another few minutes to wallow before I spur him into action.

Meanwhile, I've been following protocol. I made Bailey close his eyes so I could change into camouflage fatigues, and I've rummaged through the cabinets under the food shelves to load up my utility belt with a Glock and other doomsday must-haves such as extra ammo, matches, and a knife. The floor is littered with stuff that I've considered and rejected. Can't take it all.

216

As I'm stuffing a backpack with food and water, Bailey finally pipes up, "We don't have to go. We can stay here. It's safer."

A bottle of water slips out of my grasp and rolls across the concrete floor until it lands inside the concave drain of the hygiene station. It's like getting an accidental hole-in-one in apocalyptic mini golf. "No, Bailey, you know the plan. If there's a breach, we go through the secret passage and meet everyone at the rendezvous point in one half hour." Daddy and Logan will be there. I have faith in this.

"But what if everyone else is already dead . . . we could die out there, too."

"We could *die* in here." I mimic his tone exactly.

"Don't mock me," he scolds, glaring at me. But this is good. Anger is an emotion I can work with here. It's more active than paralyzing fear, at least.

I walk over to the mattress stack, which puts me at eye-level with his chest, and I peer up at him, though he studiously avoids my gaze. "Look, this is a secure compound, right? That means it's not grasshoppers out there threatening our lives. It's cockroaches."

"So?" He squeezes his giraffe even tighter.

"Think about it. Cockroaches are clever. Sooner or later they'll find this panic room."

"But they can't get to us in here."

"No," I agree, "they can't. So we can live here all cozied up for what? If it's just the two of us, we can maybe last a year. But what then? Cockroaches can wait us out."

"At least that year is guaranteed," he says. "If we leave, we might not last ten minutes out there."

"Nothing's guaranteed. Didn't doomsday teach you that?" I retrieve a set of fatigues in his size and hand them over. "Now get changed."

We're leaving, even if I have to drag Bailey out. Daddy's waiting. And he'll know what to do.

THEN

Holy crap. I just killed a guy. Does this mean I'm going to hell?

Daddy says no. Daddy says God understands when we kill to defend ourselves. And I trust Daddy.

But still.

Now

It's 7:30 and Logan and Daddy and his deacon gang are still M.I.A. Bailey settles deeper into the mattress, and the fatigues will probably gather dust before he walks out of here without some pretty persuasion on my part.

I'm this close to screaming in his face, but instead, I put my hand on my hip and squeeze until my fingernails break skin. "I packed your bag. Come on. We're meeting everyone in five minutes."

"They won't be there."

"They *will* be there."

"How do you know?"

"I have faith."

Bailey coughs. "You never believed in any of this. You thought your dad was crazy. And I know your secret. You never put anything in your locker."

"You're right. I didn't. But Logan did." I stalk over to Logan's locker. His combination is the same as mine. He wanted it that way, just in case. I take out his Bible and press it against my heart.

"You don't know what it's really like," Bailey says. "You sit up on your perch killing people, but you're so far removed from the actual dying. Could you look someone in the eye and slit his throat? Could you steal from someone if it meant you'd survive but he wouldn't? Could you really do what it takes to make it out there? Because I don't know if I could."

My fingernails find the tender skin of my hip again and dig in. He's right. Daddy has sheltered me from the worst. And when we leave our compound, I'll have to be as ruthless as a cockroach or risk being squashed like a grasshopper. I slide Logan's Bible into my pack. I can be ruthless.

"Look at me," I say to Bailey, and he does. Really looks at me. And for the first time, I get the sense that we are seeing each other. So I see beyond his terrified surface. I see the Bailey who repaired my "useless" red heels for me. I see the Bailey who has always let me unload on him but spared me his own trials. I see the Bailey who could give a girl a good reason to fight for survival, even if her daddy wasn't around to protect her anymore.

"We can do this." I take a deep breath, because no matter what, I want to stay alive. "If you change into those fatigues right now, I'll . . . let you kiss me."

"Really?" he asks softly, the word catching in his throat.

I nod.

I've never seen Bailey move so quickly. I watch him change, because, heck, I could be dead in five minutes, so I might as well live it up while I can. He looks fit like a swimmer under his baggy, goth clothes.

I take a semi-reluctant step towards him.

He reaches out his hands and places them on my waist. He drinks in my features like a man dying of thirst. Which, you know, he could well be in a couple of days.

"You're so beautiful," he says, and suddenly I feel myself melting under the fire in his gaze.

My lips part in an unsettling sort of anticipation.

He kisses me.

It's so freaking good, that when he pulls back slightly, I push forward to stay anchored in this moment. Why have I been avoiding Bailey all this time when we could have been doing *this*? Maybe we *could* stay here and spend our last days and months making out. Maybe we should?

"Melly," Bailey says, sighing into my mouth.

Hearing my name clears my head, and I finally break away from the kiss. I'm panting. But we *need* to go.

I take Bailey's wrist and turn it to look at the time. His pulse is racing. "It's 7:35. Time to go."

"But—"

"Come with me," I say, half sly and half shy. "And there will be more kisses like that one."

He smiles and reaches for my hand.

"Wait, one more thing," I say. I put on my tiara. "Now I'm ready."

THEN

Logan sings me a hymn. One our mom always sang to us when we couldn't sleep. "I'm sorry," he says. "I know you didn't want to kill that man."

A few tears escape, but I can't turn into a freaking waterpark attraction in front of my brother. He needs me to be a strong role model. "We're just trying to survive."

He hugs me. "It's all going to be okay."

That might be a lie. But it's a beautiful lie, isn't it?

Now

Bailey is holding my hand so tightly, I think he might legit break it. We use our free hands to feel our way carefully through the dark passage that leads out of the panic room and under the earth.

Finally, we reach the steel ladder that leads up and into our uncertain future. I take a deep breath and make the climb first. Bailey is right behind me.

At the top, I push open the trapdoor a crack and light hits my eyes. I see Daddy's eagle boots and hear his chuckle of relief.

Bailey's mother squeals his name.

And then.

"Melly!" Logan says. "You made it."

It's all going to be okay. And that's the truth. Because from now on, I'm not an ant, or a grasshopper, or a cockroach. I'm a killer queen bee.

Lenore Appelhans is the author of two dark sci-fi novels, *The Memory of After* and *Chasing Before*, a short story collection called *The Best Things in Death*, as well the humorous picture book *Chick-o-Saurus Rex*. She will graduate with an MFA in creative writing from Vermont College of Fine Arts in July 2016. Lenore loves to travel, so you can often find her on planes—at least until she learns how to teleport.

Want more? Find a Q&A with Lenore on page 264.

Lonely Hunter

Beth Revis

ENRY AWOKE TO THE SOUND of a girl crying. It was a pretty sound, melodic in a way, and he sort of wanted it to go on like a song repeated perpetually. When he cracked his eyes open, he couldn't really see who was crying, though, and when he opened his eyes all the way, she stopped.

She wasn't pretty, exactly, but she was *fierce*. She stared straight ahead at the river, her eyes flashing, a mix between angry and mournful. The red flush on her cheeks looked like flames, and Henry couldn't help but think that her beauty lay hidden within her like a soot-covered ember at the bottom of a fire.

The girl flipped half of her long auburn hair over her shoulder and glared at him as if he'd done something atrocious, which Henry hardly thought fair, considering she'd interrupted his nap with her sniffling.

"What's wrong?" Henry asked, because "Who are you?" didn't really seem like the right thing to say.

"Mmm," she growled deep in her throat. Her eyes flicked past Henry's shoulder. She looked as if she wanted to escape, but she didn't move.

The river rolled gently by them. It was calming; Henry always came here when he was upset, and it reminded him that there wasn't really anything worth being upset over. The river seemed to calm the girl, too; the flush was already fading from her pale skin, and her body relaxed into the lush moss.

Originally, the river had been intended to be something of a park for the town. The city had planned to make a mile-long walk that looped down one side, crossed a bridge, and up another. But funding for the bridge had fallen through before the path had even been paved, so rather than making a loop, the trail ended abruptly in the woods. The children's playground at the entrance of the park had been completed, and few people ever made it to the end of the trail, much less beyond, deeper into the forest where there was nothing but moss and trees and water.

That was the part of the river park Henry liked — the places where no one else went. He'd certainly never woken up to a crying girl here before.

"I'm Henry."

"Ren."

Henry opened his mouth to speak, a smile playing on his lips, but before he had a chance, Ren said, "R-e-n. Not like the bird."

Henry did laugh then. "I was just about to say that." She didn't speak; she just stared at him with eyes that seemed to know more about him than they should. "So," he said to break the silence, "why were you upset?"

"Pardon?"

"You were crying."

"Oh." Ren brushed her hand vaguely through the air. Whatever had been making her cry was clearly not important now. "Look," she added. "Let's just sit here. The sun is setting, and the river's like a song."

Henry blinked. She filled his senses and fogged his mind. He'd only just met her, he knew nothing about her but her name, but the image of her face turned toward the orange glow of the sun reflected on the bubbling river poured into his memory so completely that he knew he would never forget this moment with this girl.

"Oh, bloody hell," Ren growled. She leapt onto her feet, snapping her arm out at the elbow so that her hand flew out in front of her.

Only her hand kept going, faster and faster, across the river. No, that wasn't right. Her hand was still attached to her arm. But an imprint of her hand, a red outline like the one that could be left across your face if you're slapped had sprung from her palm and flown like a spear over the water. Red. Orangey-red. *Fire.* She'd shot fire from her hand.

The flame exploded on the other bank, a firework of sparks and moss and dirt and . . . something else. Something black. And rusty-crimson. Outlined briefly but terrifying against the shadows of the trees.

"What the—?!" Henry shouted, scrambling back.

"LEAVE. ME. ALONE!" Ren screamed.

"All right," Henry said, his eyes wide. He took several steps away from her.

"Not you!" Ren shouted without turning around. "YOU!" she screamed, flinging her arm out once more and sending another hand of fire across the river. Something else exploded, something that Henry could only see for a bright, shining moment as it disintegrated.

Ren took a deep breath in and expelled it slowly. Although her shoulders relaxed, when she turned around Henry could still see the fire in her eyes.

"What the hell—?" Henry started.

Ren sank to the ground, her arms hanging limply to her sides, her legs tucked under her. "Just . . . go away," she said. "Can't you see that you should leave? Isn't it obvious?"

"It's obvious that there's some really screwed up things going on," Henry said. "What the hell was that?"

"My problem," Ren said, still not looking up at him. "Not yours."

She looked so . . . so broken then. This girl had just shot *fire* from her hands, fighting something Henry saw only in the moment of its death, but that moment had been enough.

He sat down opposite her. He opened his mouth. He closed it. He realized that what was needed were her words, not his.

And he also realized that he deeply cared to hear them. He'd just met this girl; he had no reason to give her a second thought at all, regardless of whether or not she could shoot fire from her hands. It wasn't curiosity that made him want to stay beside her, although he was of course curious. There was some deeper emotion stirring inside him, something he couldn't quite name. His ex-girlfriend used to go on and on about love at first sight, but that was never something Henry had felt. Not with her, and not with Ren, either. This feeling wasn't love. But it was . . . it was a string. He felt like he was tied to her, and to walk away now, to sever that imaginary string between them, felt wrong. His emotion for her wasn't something he could name, it wasn't something tangible at all, but it kept him in place, beside her, waiting.

"They're demons," she said softly, finally.

"Demons." Henry tried to keep the doubt from his voice.

"Demons."

"Invisible demons."

Ren barked out a laugh. "They're not invisible to me. Just you."

"Just me. So everyone on Earth is walking around seeing invisible demons but me."

She smiled this time, a real smile. "Okay, so I'm one of the few that can see them."

"And fight them."

She looked down at her hand, the one that had shot fire and destroyed the . . . whatever it was. The demon. She concentrated on her palm, but her gaze was passive, as if it was nothing more than a weapon that only vaguely interested her. "So, look," she said eventually, daring to meet his eyes again. "That's me. I'm a demon hunter. Which sounds crazy, but it's true."

"Clearly."

"And I'm sort of like a magnet. I have magic, and they want it, so they're always showing up around me. Which means if you're around me, you're going to be around demons."

"At least I can't see them."

"But they can hurt you. And you will see them eventually."

He looked at her curiously.

"Magic rubs off," she said. "If you stay close to someone with magic, like me, you'll catch it too."

"Like the flu."

"Yes," she said, smirking. "But with considerably different symptoms."

"Such as seeing demons and shooting fire from your hands."

"Better than shooting fire from other places."

Henry cracked a smile at that, but it evaporated quickly. He had seen only a flash of the demon before it disintegrated, and that moment had been horrific. But how much more terrible could it have been had he seen it in more detail, seen it while alive and not already turning to ash?

And more to the point: "Why are you telling me all this?" he asked, suspicion rising in his voice.

Ren's eyes didn't waver as she met Henry's gaze, but it took her a long time to answer him. "I guess..." she said eventually, "I'm just tired. Of no one else knowing about me." She paused again. "Of being alone."

While Henry didn't think she was lying, he wasn't sure she was telling the whole truth either. Why tell her biggest secrets to a stranger?

"But you're right," Ren continued. "It's selfish of me, using you as a confessional. And because just like the demons are drawn to my magic, it'll influence you, too, or anyone who stays close to me. Stick around me and you'll get powers, too, not just to see the demons, but to fight them."

Something inside Henry's body did a weird sort of twitch, his stomach dropping and his heart rising to his throat. This seemed overwhelmingly fast and utterly unbelievable, but . . . he had seen something of the magic and the demons and the truth in this girl's eyes, this girl he'd just barely met. But who already seemed . . . special to him. It was a weird word to apply to a girl who he barely knew, but it was true nevertheless. She was already someone that he seemed to understand, that was important to him.

"And this," Ren said very, very seriously, "is why you should go."

"Go?"

"Leave. You never should have seen me fight a demon in the first place. You were in the wrong place at the wrong time. Just go. Forget about me."

Henry laughed. "I really doubt I could ever forget about you."

This, for whatever reason, was entirely the wrong thing for him to have said. The angry red flush rose in Ren's cheeks again, and her hands curled up into fists.

"No, really," she said, her voice low and dangerous. "It's not worth it. I'm sorry you saw what you saw and I shouldn't have said anything, but I did. You did, and I did. But it stops now. It's not . . . it's not worth it," she repeated, but there was doubt in her voice now.

Henry stared at this strange girl, and he wondered just what it was that hurt her so very much. "Why don't I . . ." He paused, knowing he had only this one chance to talk to her. "Why don't I just stick around a little right now?" he said. She was obviously upset, and who could blame her? She had just turned a demon to dust. "No strings," Henry added. "Just . . . we can just sit here for now."

She snorted like she didn't believe him.

But he didn't go away. And she didn't either. And they sat there, together, as the river bubbled by and the sky turned into stars.

* * *

When Henry finally stood up to go, Ren grabbed his wrist. "You can't tell anyone, you know."

Henry tried to laugh it off. "As if anyone would believe me."

"No." Her grip tightened. "You don't understand. It doesn't matter if no one would believe you. You still can't tell. You can't tell anyone."

"Why?"

A dark look passed over Ren's face. "If you tell," she said, "then I would have to use my magic to do something I don't want to do."

Henry didn't ask, but he knew the confusion showed on his face.

"I would have to erase memories," she said. "I hate doing that."

"You've done it before?"

Ren nodded. "More than once," she said evenly, as if she were trying to control her voice. "I hate it every time."

"Okay," Henry said. His eyes held her clear gray gaze. "I promise. I won't tell anyone."

His words seemed to be enough to satisfy her.

"So . . ." He let his voice trail off. "Same time, same place tomorrow?"

Her face fell into a mask. "It was nice to meet you, Henry," she said somewhat coldly.

And then she walked away.

* * *

But she was there by the river, waiting for him, the very next day.

The river became their daily meeting place. He had no idea where she lived, no idea where she went when they separated. But the river was theirs.

Ren and Henry spent most of their days alone, together. Just them and, sometimes, a demon.

The first three times, he never even saw the demons. One minute Ren was talking to him, the next she was shooting fire from her hands and cursing like a sailor under her breath while little wisps of smoke spurted out of thin air. The fourth time Henry was almost hurt; he saw a flicker of a shadow and paused, and something dark flew so close to his face that it singed his hair.

The fifth time, he saw the demon.

But before that, he told Ren he loved her.

It happened like this.

Before he'd met Ren, Henry had spent most of his life empty. He'd never have described it like that, but now that he knew what it was like to have a full life, he could think of no other way to describe life before Ren than empty.

Ren made things exciting. Not just because she was a demon hunter, but because her very presence made the world around her light up. She laughed at rain; she cursed at wind. She cried when she wanted to cry, but she always found something to smile about even before the tears had dried from her eyes. She questioned everything; she noticed things about the world that Henry had never noticed before.

They had some silly conversation after another, interspersed with something serious and real. She would wonder aloud if everyone saw color the same way, if the purple she saw was the same as the purple Henry saw, and then she'd wonder if there were any other people like her, people with magic who saw demons, who maybe fought them or maybe joined them, but either way, they never contacted her. She was alone.

But before Henry could say anything to her, she skipped away, babbling about how her magic can't be so bad if it could make s'mores, and Henry couldn't help but laugh at her sudden whimsy. When he laughed, she laughed too. And then they weren't laughing, they were just looking at each other, and the moon was shining big and bright, and there was just a hint of stars in the sky, and Henry couldn't help himself, his mouth just opened up and the words tumbled out.

"I love you."

"Son of a—"

Henry blinked. That wasn't exactly the response he'd expected.

"They're here," Ren hissed. She shot a hand of fire over Henry's shoulder. Henry turned. That's when he saw a demon for the first time. Really saw it, fully, not just a shadow, but an actual thing living and breathing and hating in front of him.

It was more horrible than he had ever thought it could be.

He gagged when he saw it; his eyes swam and his stomach churned bile.

Imagine a hamburger that's been cooked on a grill too quickly. The outside is black and crisp, but if you press down on it with the spatula, then bright red meat bursts through the cracks in the burnt outside. That is what the demon's flesh was like, except sometimes instead of red, raw meat bursting from the cracked, crispy skin there was pale green pus, or yellow curdled fat, or something gray that steamed when it dripped from the body onto the cool night ground. It had teeth everywhere, bursting from every angle in its mouth, cutting through its own snarling lips, emerging from the cheekbones like hard, white, sharp pimples—there was even one fang that curled down from the corner of its blood-red eye like a cavity-filled tear. The monster had only fingers, no thumbs, but there were at least twelve fingers in a circle all around the hand, and on each finger was a curling, yellowed claw that was cracked and caked with dried blood and something brown and crumbly.

When it walked, the earth shook. When it twitched its scaly tail, the grass died. When it breathed, the air turned sour. And when it looked back at Henry looking at him, it made Henry want to run and hide.

The foul thing smiled at him, and laughed, and Henry noticed that it even had teeth on its tongue.

Henry whimpered.

Ren leapt up from the demon she'd just slain, and threw Henry back with one arm as she slung the other one out in front of her and sent a hand of flame straight at the demon. The hand print scorched into the monster's burnt flesh, turning the center of his chest into a bright five-fingered outline before the demon exploded. A wisp of black smoke rose up from where the hand of fire had been while chunks of dismembered demon flesh dropped haphazardly on the ground.

"You okay?" Ren asked, panting.

Henry nodded mutely. A piece of the thing's face landed on his shoulder, oozing pus onto his jacket. Had this happened before? When Ren attacked the demons when they were still invisible, he'd never seen their effects, never felt or smelled or experienced them. But now they were here, not just visible but *present* in an overwhelming way he had never expected.

Ren reached up and flicked it off. Henry stared at the slimy trail it left on the cloth.

"I . . . I didn't know they exploded like that."

"What'd you think they did?"

"I dunno. Just . . . disappeared. All I used to see was a bit of smoke."

Ren nodded. Her eyes were very serious, her mouth a grim line.

They just stood there, neither of them looking at each other. The bits of demon hissed and steamed, quickly burning into the ground and disintegrating. The smell, however, did not evaporate so easily.

"Let's get out of here," Ren said. She reached for Henry.

He jerked away. "I . . . um. I need to go for a walk."

Ren nodded, but Henry didn't notice. He didn't turn around as he walked deeper into the forest, trailing along the edge of the river.

His sneakers skidded on the slick green moss, and Henry dropped to his knees by the river.

He had never imagined it would be so disgusting. Even though the calming waters were right in front of him, all he could see was the drip of blood on the demon's fangs as it had grinned at him.

He gasped for air; his eyes watered.

Something nearby laughed.

Henry's head jerked up.

This demon was smaller than the other had been, more sinewy. It didn't have an excess of teeth. It had an excess of arms and hands. There were the two in the shoulder were they should be, but two more sprouted out from its rib cage, and four reached over the shoulders from the back. And all the hands, all eight of them, were

236

scrabbling across the mossy green earth toward Henry's crouched and tired body.

Henry shouted and jumped back. Without thinking, he threw his hands in front of his face.

A white-hot feeling jerked from his stomach and out, out, through his chest, his arms, his hands . . . and a flame burst from his palms and into the demon.

The demon looked down at its chest once, then looked up, surprised, then exploded.

"HENRY!" Ren screamed, racing through the trees down the slope toward him. "Are you all right?"

Henry nodded. He felt sick. The demon—what was left of him—twitched on the ground, but it was already dead.

"You did it." Ren sounded amazed. "Magic. You've not been with me that long; you're very powerful."

"Is that why the demon came after me?" Henry asked. He had not intended his voice to be so sharp.

Ren nodded, but there was something cautious about her eyes. "Yes. They are attracted to magic. You've got some now."

"I don't think I want it."

Ren stopped—everything about her seemed to pause, even her breath. "It's . . . it's not something I can help. As long as you're around me, then you'll get magic."

"Oh."

Neither of them spoke for a long time.

"You don't want to be around me anymore, do you?" Ren finally asked.

Henry looked from the corpse of the demon into Ren's eyes.

"No," he said simply. He could feel the connection he had felt between them being pulled taut, threatening to break. He loved the feeling of being near her, the fullness and the excitement, the promise of something more. But he feared her and a future beside her even more.

Silent tears were already streaming down Ren's face.

"I thought, maybe . . . You got the magic so much sooner this time; you were so much more willing to join me this time . . . But don't worry. It will go away again. When I go away too."

This time? Henry thought. "This time?" he said.

Ren raised her hand and pressed it against Henry's forehead. "This time," she said, a wry grin bursting up through the salty flood of her tears. "Forget," she said. "Forget." There was magic in her voice.

Henry's eyes rolled up into his head. His legs crumbled under him; he dropped with a muted thud against the moss. Only the river made a sound as Ren bent down and pulled Henry's legs into a more natural position. He looked like he was napping. Peaceful, blissful ignorance spread across his face.

Ren tried to stop looking, she tried to stop crying, she tried to leave. She was actually able to take a few steps away from him before she, too, fell to the ground and gave way to her sobs.

* * *

Henry awoke to the sound of a girl crying. It was a pretty sound, melodic in a way, and he sort of wanted it to go on like a song repeated perpetually. When he cracked his eyes open, he couldn't really see who was crying, though, and when he opened his eyes all the way, she stopped.

"Who are you?" Henry asked. The girl was beautiful in the moonlight; her tears made her more beautiful. "I'm Henry," he added when the girl didn't say anything.

The girl stood up abruptly and walked away. Her feet were light; she was almost running. Before Henry had a chance to call out to her, though, she stopped. When she turned around, there was a look of defeat in her eyes, and one last tear.

"I'm Ren."

Beth Revis is the *NY Times* bestselling author of the *Across the Universe* series. The complete trilogy is now available in more than 20 languages. A native of North Carolina, Beth is also the author of the new science fiction novel for teens, *The Body Electric,* as well as several science fiction short stories.

Want more? Find a Q&A with Beth on page 266.

Author Q&As

Q&A with Gretchen McNeil

What was your inspiration for "The Eyes Have It?"

I wanted to play on the way our eyes can deceive us, both within the context of the story, and in terms of the inter-character relationships.

How is writing short stories different than writing a novel?

Short stories are a snippet in time, a moment, a tone poem, a brief glimpse into the window of a moving train. For me, they're like a quick, impactful jab as opposed to the ten-round match that is a full novel.

What's next for you?

My next YA horror novel *Relic* will be out with Harper Impulse in March 2016, followed by my first YA contemporary *I'm Not Your Manic Pixie Dream Girl* with Balzer + Bray in the fall of 2016.

Q&A with Kate Karyus Quinn

What was your inspiration for "The One True Miranda Lieu"?

My main inspiration was the amazing movie, *The Truman Show*. I really loved the idea of playing around with a character who has lived in this world that seems false and odd in so many ways, but for them it's the only truth they've ever known. This set-up gave me a chance to write my favorite type of character—those that are a little bit broken, but who find a core of strength inside themselves.

What food/beverage would be a good pairing with your short story?

A tall glass of pink lemonade would go perfectly with "The One True Miranda Lieu." First of all, pink plays a rather important role in this story. And the mixture of tart and sweet is much like the town that Miranda calls home.

What's next for you?

My next YA novel is *Down With The Shine*. The book centers around Lennie Cash, an outcast who decides to crash the biggest party of the school year. She brings several bottles of her Uncles' notorious moonshine to pass around, along with their one-of-a-kind party toast asking drinkers to "make a wish." The next morning Lennie finds out that every single crazy drunken wish was granted. *Down With The Shine* will be available from HarperTeen in 2016!

Also by Kate Karyus Quinn

Another Little Piece
(Don't You) Forget About Me

Find more about Kate at
www.katekaryusquinn.com!

Q&A with Justina Ireland

What was your inspiration for "Such a Lovely Monster"?

The monster that lives under my bed. He's a real pain, but he comes in handy every now and then. For example: when looking for a topic for a short story.

How is writing short stories different than writing a novel?

There are less words.

What stories do you like to read?

All of them. I mostly read Science Fiction and Fantasy, though.

What food/beverage would be a good pairing with your short story?

Root beer and pepperoni pizza. It goes well with murder.

What's next for you?

I'm going to go eat breakfast. Alas, it will not be root beer and pepperoni pizza, though. But there may be some murder involved.

Also by Justina Ireland

Vengeance Bound
Promise of Shadows

Find more about Justina at www.justinaireland.com!

Q&A with Kelly Fiore

What was your inspiration for "Heroin(e)"?

Baltimore has gotten a lot of attention in the news recently, and for good reason. But my story takes place in a different part of that city—or, rather, with a different focus. The heroin epidemic in Baltimore is something that can't be exaggerated or dramatized because it is brutal. It is also NOT a problem relegated to the lower-income sectors of the city—it hits high school students and nurses and teachers and mothers. There are people addicted to heroin who never smoked marijuana or a cigarette. Heroin is a spin-off epidemic of the opiate dependency of our country and my story is a small window into that, I hope.

What's next for you?

My first YA novel with HarperTeen, *Thicker Than Water*, comes out in January 2016. This book is completely different than my other YA novels—it's the story of siblings, one of whom is addicted to OxyContin, and how those siblings ultimately navigate their relationship, even after one of them is dead.

Also by Kelly Fiore

Just Like the Movies
Taste Test
Thicker Than Water

**Find more about Kelly at
www.kellyfiorewrites.com!**

Q&A with Demitria Lunetta

What was your inspiration for "Canary"?

A lot of the stories I think up are speculative fiction, which means that they are filled with fantastical elements that could never happen. For "Canary," I wanted to write a horror story that could happen, set in the real world. Although a family living undisturbed by outside influences for a hundred years is unlikely, the evil that people are capable of is very real.

What stories do you like to read?

Everything! But especially sci-fi, fantasy, and historical fiction.

What food/beverage would be a good pairing with your short story?

Oreos!

What's next for you?

My next YA novel is *Bad Blood* about a 16-year-old girl haunted by dreams and compelled to cut herself until she discovers a family secret and a past full of magic that could both save her and put her in mortal danger. It's set in Scotland and will be out from Delacorte in Spring of 2017.

Also by Demitria Lunetta

In the After
In the End

**Find more about Demitria at
demitrialunetta.blogspot.com!**

Q&A with Mindy McGinnis

What was your inspiration for "Phantom Heart"?

I find myself going down rabbit holes on the internet quite often, and was reading about phantom limb syndrome. I was thinking that having an unscratchable itch would have to be the most horrible thing ever, and it led to me wondering what it would be like to have a phantom heart, and feel love and loss that doesn't belong to you. Then I thought—"OH! Story idea!"

How is writing short stories different than writing a novel?

I find it much more challenging. You have less space to build a world, create empathy for a non-existent person, build a plot, and execute an ending. It's a different type of writing, and one that in many ways takes more skill, in my opinion.

What food/beverage would be a good pairing with your short story?

Raw meat (but don't do that, you'll get sick).

What's next for you?

I have a Gothic historical thriller set in an insane asylum—*A Madness So Discreet*—coming from Katherine Tegen on October 6, 2015!

Also by Mindy McGinnis

Not a Drop to Drink
In a Handful of Dust
A Madness So Discreet

**Find more about Mindy at
www.mindymcginnis.com!**

Q&A with
Joelle Charbonneau

What was your inspiration for "Reunion"?

You know, I've always been fascinated with families. No one can hurt you more or make you do crazy things like family. I guess I wanted to explore what happens when love and hate really are so closely intertwined.

What stories do you like to read?

I like to read anything with a mystery or puzzle involved. I am a sucker for puzzles!

What food/beverage would be a good pairing with your short story?

Hot chocolate—because I think hot chocolate goes with everything!

What's next for you?

My next book hitting shelves is a social media thriller called *Need*. It comes out November 3, 2015. You'll find me hiding under my bed until then.

Also by Joelle Charbonneau

The Testing
Independent Study
Graduation Day
Need

Find more about Joelle at
www.joellecharbonneau.com!

Q&A with
Geoffrey Girard

What was your inspiration for "Not Fade Away"?

While visiting a family member at a retirement community, one of the residents (a total stranger) caught my eye and waved me over. I said hello and he mumbled something. When I leaned in closer, he said it again: "They're gonna burn it to the ground." And that's it. Not another word or explanation followed. Perfect story prompt. The other ingredient is that we've been studying existentialism in class this quarter (I teach high school English) and issues of life's monotony, and *ennui*, came up a lot. A feeling people of all ages sometimes have.

What stories do you like to read?
On my nightstand now is an excellent collection by speculative writer Chesya Burke. Vonnegut, Bradbury, Lovecraft, James Joyce, Kelly Link, Hemingway, Shirley Jackson, David Foster Wallace, Robert E. Howard . . . are collections I read again and again.

What food/beverage would be a good pairing with your short story?

Apple juice.

Also by Geoffrey Girard

Project Cain

**Find more about Geoffrey at
www.geoffreygirard.com!**

Q&A with Lydia Kang

What was your inspiration for "Blàrach Bridge"?

Procrastination! I was online and saw one of those lists. You know, the "Top Ten Things You Do When You're Supposed to be Working" type of lists that waste time. Except this one was "Top Ten Most Haunted Places on Earth." It got my attention. Overtoun Bridge in Scotland was mentioned. When I found out that there was a place where dogs leapt to their death for unknown reasons, I knew someday I'd turn it into a dark story.

How is writing short stories different than writing a novel?

With a novel, you have pages and pages to develop a character, stakes, relationships, and a character development arc. In a short story, you have such a tight economy of words to do the same. It's a huge challenge.

258

What food/beverage would be a good pairing with your short story?

Classic Indian desserts, of course. (This only makes sense if you read the story!)

Also by Lydia Kang

Control
Catalyst

**Find more about Lydia at
www.lydiakang.com!**

Q&A with R.C. Lewis

What was your inspiration for "Chasing the Sky"?

I was watching a crime drama where people were using children as bombers and started thinking about situations where maybe the children's parents weren't the real monsters.

How is writing short stories different than writing a novel?

For me, at least, I like short stories to leave a little more open to the imagination. Things are hinted at just enough for the reader to make inferences and may not be very spelled out. That can also make it tricky, because there still needs to be enough detail that the story holds together and makes some sense.

What stories do you like to read?

I'm trying to branch out and read new types of stories when I can, but I always come back to sci-fi and fantasy.

260

On the sci-fi front, the more mind-twisting it is, the better I like it.

What's next for you?

My YA sci-fi *Spinning Starlight* is a sci-fi take (very broadly!) on Hans Christian Andersen's "The Wild Swans" and comes out October 6, 2015. I've also got a couple of other things in the works—one sci-fi, one contemporary.

Also by R.C. Lewis

Stitching Snow
Spinning Starlight

Find more about R.C. at
www.rclewisbooks.com!

Q&A with Phoebe North

What was your inspiration for "The Cowbird Egg"?

I wrote "The Cowbird Egg" while I was still in graduate school (years ago now!). My now-husband was visiting and I woke to him hogging the blankets in my rather small bed. "You're a cowbird egg, pushing me out!" I joked, and then realized that there was a whole story there, just waiting to be written.

How is writing short stories different than writing a novel?

When I write short stories I like to do it all in one rush, spending two or three days churning out words. I write them rarely, but intensely. Writing novels is more of a slog, slow, steady.

What stories do you like to read?

Kelly Link!

What food/beverage would be a good pairing with your short story?

All your favorite junk food. Everlasting Gobstoppers, Chuckles, Good & Plenty.

What's next for you?

I plan to transcend my mortal flesh, or take a shower, whichever comes first.

Also by Phoebe North

Starglass
Starbreak
Stardawn

Find more about Phoebe at
www.phoebenorth.com!

Q&A with Lenore Appelhans

What was your inspiration for "Panic Room"?

"Panic Room" started with a voice—that first line of the piece: "I'm, like, such a murderer." Here was a girl in conflict and she wanted to tell her story. I'm sure I was influenced by a million little things, but I think one of the big questions I wanted to explore was how much is a person willing—and able—to give up in order to survive? How much light do you need in order to make it through the darkness?

What food/beverage would be a good pairing with your short story?

To really get in tune with the atmosphere of the story, you'd have to get some of those cheap, bulk canned foods and some bottled water. But there is mention of ice cream, too, so if the bleakness of industrial peas doesn't appeal, settle in with a scoop of sweetness instead.

Q&A with Beth Revis

What was your inspiration for "Lonely Hunter"?

I think it was a combination of too much sweet and not enough bitter in what I'd been reading lately. I can only handle so much Disney (which I love!) before I have to write something with blood. Or, in this case, pus-dripping demons.

How is writing short stories different than writing a novel?

Because it's such a short medium, you have to strip away everything that doesn't directly touch upon the characters' immediate problems. It's like a haiku—there's only room for the essence.

What stories do you like to read?

Ones with a twist, from O. Henry to Isaac Asimov.

What food/beverage would be a good pairing with your short story?

Absinthe—it's green like the moss by the river, and also makes you forget everything you've done while drinking it.

What's next for you?

A new novel coming in summer of 2016!

Also by Beth Revis

Across the Universe
A Million Suns
Shades of Earth
The Body Electric
The Future Collection

Find more about Beth at
www.bethrevis.com!

Acknowledgments

The editors would like to thank Deanna M. Piña, Adriann Ranta, Beth Revis, R.C. Lewis, and Alexander Lunetta for making *Among the Shadows* possible, along with all of the generous people who donated to our anthology on Kickstarter.

CPSIA information can be obtained
at www.ICGtesting.com
Printed in the USA
FSOW03n1142210317
32160FS